"Instead of avoiding each other, we start spending time together."

Her stomach did a quick spin and dip. "And that solves...what?"

"It gets us used to each other again," he said. "Accustomed to being together and *not* giving in to the heat between us. With any luck, after some time passes, that'll cool off."

Not from where she was standing. Just having him in her office was lighting up her insides and making her blood burn and bubble. "You think so?"

"I do. We keep our hands off each other, but hang out and we'll get past this...need."

"Seems risky."

"I can do it if you can."

A challenge. He'd always known the way to get to her. Tell Beth she *couldn't* do something and she would find a way to accomplish it. "Why couldn't I? You're not completely irresistible, Camden."

That was a lie, because, yes, he was.

* * *

The Price of Passion by Maureen Child is part of the Texas Cattleman's Club: Rags to Riches series.

Dear Reader,

Here we are again, back in Royal, Texas, one of my favorite spots!

And as it turns out, Camden Guthrie and Beth Wingate have become two of my favorite characters. After being gone fifteen years, Cam is back in Royal and Beth is not happy about it. The history they share is brought back to life almost instantly.

But along with the passion comes the memory of betrayal and the reminder that once trust is lost, it's hard to regain. Constantly thrown together, Beth and Cam have to find a way to work with each other.

To build a future, they must face the past and everything that brings with it. But family loyalties are being tested. As rumors race through Royal, Beth and Cam turn to each other and, together, they decide to pay whatever price passion demands.

I really hope you enjoy reading this book as much as I did writing it. Being in Royal, Texas, is always a pleasure and being able to share these visits with you makes it even more special!

Happy reading,

Maureen Child

MAUREEN CHILD

THE PRICE OF PASSION

Special thanks and acknowledgment are given to Maureen Child for her contribution to the Texas Cattleman's Club: Rags to Riches miniseries.

Recycling programs for this product may not exist in your area.

ISBN-13: 978-1-335-20913-9

The Price of Passion

This edition published by arrangement with Harlequin Books S.A.

For questions and comments about the quality of this book, please contact us at CustomerService@Harlequin.com.

Harlequin Enterprises ULC
22 Adelaide St. West, 40th Floor
Toronto, Ontario M5H 4E3, Canada
www.Harlequin.com

Printed in U.S.A.

Maureen Child writes for the Harlequin Desire line and can't imagine a better job. A seven-time finalist for the prestigious Romance Writers of America RITA® Award, Maureen is the author of more than one hundred romance novels. Her books regularly appear on bestseller lists and have won several awards, including a Prism Award, a National Readers' Choice Award, a Colorado Romance Writers Award of Excellence and a Golden Quill Award. She is a native Californian but has recently moved to the mountains of Utah.

Books by Maureen Child

Harlequin Desire

Rich Rancher's Redemption
Billionaire's Bargain
Tempt Me in Vegas
Bombshell for the Boss
Red Hot Rancher
Jet Set Confessions
The Price of Passion

Visit her Author Profile page at Harlequin.com, or maureenchild.com, for more titles.

You can also find Maureen Child on Facebook, along with other Harlequin Desire authors, at Facebook.com/harlequindesireauthors!

For my mom, Sallye Carberry,
because she introduced me to the
magical world of reading...which eventually
led me here! Thanks, Mom.

One

Nothing much had changed in Royal, Texas.

And Camden Guthrie was glad to see it. Sure, the town was a little bigger than he remembered and there were some new shops, but it was still the place where he'd grown up. Cam was only just beginning to realize how much he'd missed it. He'd been in self-imposed exile in Southern California.for fifteen years, and now every breath of warm Texas air felt like a homecoming.

Damned if he'd ever leave again.

"Cam?"

He turned and smiled at the sheriff. Nathan Battles was older, so they hadn't hung out much as kids, but no one was a stranger in a small town.

"Good to see you, Nate." Cam held out a hand and Nate took it in a firm shake.

"I heard you bought the old Circle K ranch."

"Of course you did." Cam shook his head. Gossip was the lifeblood of small towns, and Royal was no different. And, given that Nate's wife Amanda owned and ran the Royal Diner—basically ground zero for information exchanges—she probably kept him up-to-date on whatever she heard.

Nate grinned. "You want secrets? Don't use Natalie Barnes as your real estate agent. She's been telling everyone who will listen that you bought the ranch where you and your folks used to work."

Cam nodded at the reminder. The Circle K had been a huge part of his life. His parents had both worked as horse trainers for the owner, and Cam, as a kid, had done whatever needed doing—from feeding the animals to mucking out stalls and carpentry work.

He had a lot of good memories of that place—along with some he'd worked hard to forget. Like the loss of his parents in a stable fire when he was seventeen. Bad wiring had started it, and his mother and father had been so determined to free the stalled horses that they'd been trapped inside when the roof finally collapsed.

But the ranch had remained his home. He'd continued to live and work there while he finished school. Two years ago, when he'd decided to come back to Royal, Cam had made an offer on the property, and when it was accepted he'd figured it was fate. Sort of coming full circle.

Now that he was back, he had a lot of ideas for improvements on the ranch and plenty of plans for its future. *His* future. A future he'd once believed would include Beth Wingate.

Damn. Even thinking her name had his blood racing. Fifteen years since he'd seen her. Fifteen years since he'd touched her. Yet, Beth was there. Always. In his mind. In a dark, locked-up corner of his heart.

"Yeah," he finally said in response to Nate. "It's good to be back."

He wondered, though, if he'd feel the same once he'd seen Beth again.

Just thinking about her now could bring up so many mixed emotions. He buried them all because how the hell could he sort through them? He hadn't come back to Royal for her. He'd come because this was his place. His home. Texas was in his blood, and Royal was his heartbeat. Over the years he'd silenced the urge to come home. He and his late wife, Julie, had built a life and a fortune in California, but always there had been the ache for Texas. Now he was back, and nothing would make him leave.

Not even the one woman who still haunted him.

Nate pulled the brim of his gray hat down lower over his eyes. "I hear you're stocking some Longhorns on your ranch, along with the Black Angus."

Cam laughed. "You hear plenty."

"I do." The sheriff gave him a shameless grin. "And I'm glad if it's true. The Longhorn is pure Texas. It's good you're doing what you can to help the breed survive."

He had bigger plans than just the Longhorns, but Cam wasn't ready to let anyone else in on what he had in mind. Still, the thought of what was in the works made him smile.

"Well, it is true. I've got a small herd of a few hundred arriving end of the week." Cam was finally living the dream he'd had since he was a kid. His own ranch. Run his way. "We'll be keeping them separate from the Angus. Don't want any crossbreeding."

Nate laughed. "Better you than me. Riding herd on the town is enough excitement for me."

Cam nodded and glanced around Main Street again. It was a quiet town and, he thought, a little bigger than he remembered it. The closest large city was Dallas, but here in Royal was everything anyone could need. County buildings crouched around a park with tidy flower beds, live oaks and manicured grass. Along the street were restaurants, a bank and dozens of shops—everything from hardware to hair salons.

The sidewalks were bustling but not crowded, and that was a relief. In Southern California, you practically had to lock yourself in a closet if you wanted some space for yourself.

Now, in the first week of June, summer was just a promise and the humidity hadn't quite reached air-conditioning-or-die level yet.

"I wanted to tell you," Nate was saying, "I was real sorry to hear about Julie."

Pain, sharp and swift, stabbed at Cam, stole his breath and then slowly slipped away again. He'd come to grips with the death of his wife two years ago. It was losing Julie that had finally convinced him to come back to Royal. But when he was reminded of it out of the blue, it could still hit him hard.

"Thanks, Nate. I appreciate it." Polite but cool, letting his old friend know without saying that Cam didn't want to talk about it.

Nate got the message. Nodding, he said, "Well, I'm guessing you've got a lot to do here in town. I'll let you get to it."

"Yeah, I'm headed to the bank." Had to open a new account and arrange for his money to be wired here from LA.

"I'm headed back to the office, but let's get together soon. Tell some lies."

Cam grinned. Relieved to be back on solid ground, he said, "Sounds good."

He watched the sheriff walk away and envied him for a moment. Nathan Battles had always known his place. He had found it years ago, and now he walked through Royal, a man at peace with himself and the life he'd carved out.

Cam was back in Royal to do the same.

It took him nearly a half hour to walk to the bank because he was stopped every few feet by old friends. Back in California, he was a successful businessman. A self-made millionaire. But in Royal, Texas, he was a home-grown success story. People being people, they were all curious about what he'd been doing the last fifteen years. And these people, being Texans, would want their questions answered.

Funny, because back in the day, he'd been the half–Native American son of ranch workers, and his only claim to fame was starring on the Royal High School baseball team. Back then, he'd had major-league dreams that fueled his imagination. Cam had gotten scholarship offers based on his pitching abilities, but he hadn't taken any of them because his world had been abruptly upended after graduation.

Yet here he was, returning to his hometown a millionaire many times over and the owner of the very ranch where his late parents had worked. Life could be strange—even when it was satisfying.

He walked into the bank and paused, taking it in. A big building with the stamp of Texas all over it, there were wide red tiles on the floor, paintings of Texas on the walls and dark wooden beams on the ceiling. The counters were of gleaming dark wood to match those beams, and the tellers worked behind a wall of thick plexiglass. There were several manned desks opposite the tellers and a staircase leading to the second floor in the corner. Cam's gaze swept the desks, looking for the bank manager. But when he spotted him, it wasn't the man Cam focused on, but the woman sitting opposite him.

Beth Wingate.

Every ounce of breath rushed from his lungs, and his vision narrowed until she was all he could see. It was as if the world had disappeared, leaving her in a bright spotlight.

Cam couldn't have looked away if it had meant his life. Because at one time she had *been* his life. And, apparently, his body remembered. He was hard as stone, his breath laboring, his heart racing. His palms itched to touch her again, and even as he silently admitted that simple fact, guilt rushed into his mind to tear him a new one.

Hell, his wife had only been dead two years, and here he was lusting after the woman who had ripped out his heart and pushed him into Julie's arms.

As if she could *feel* him looking at her, Beth slowly turned her head and fixed her gaze on his.

Her eyes were filled with memory as his own must have been. Once upon a time, he'd thought the world began and ended in those green eyes. Now he felt the power of her gaze slamming into his chest like a punch to the solar plexus. Why did she still have to be so damn beautiful? Her hair fell long and straight to the middle of her back, still blond but with highlights now that made it shimmer like gold when she shook her head. She was tall and thin, but not so skinny she didn't have curves that he remembered all too well. As he watched, she stood up and held herself like a damn queen.

He should be irritated by that, because of course she did. She was a Wingate, and in Royal they were at the top of the ladder. Hell, Beth's mother, Ava, had been the interior designer of the Texas Cattleman's Club, and there was no club that better described Royal. The TCC was renowned for its membership. Every wealthy, influential person in this corner of Texas was a member, and those who weren't were trying to get in. As Camden would be.

Beth stood there staring at him, and he let his gaze drag up and down her body lazily. She wore a summer dress, sleeveless, in a dusty blue with pale yellow stripes. Her tanned legs were bare, and she wore three-inch heeled sandals on her narrow feet.

She looked…too damn good. And he probably looked like just what he was—a man struck dumb by lust and need. Why the hell had he run into her in a public place? Knowing Royal, everyone in the bank was watching this meeting. Waiting to see if there would be a fight, or fireworks of a different kind.

There would be neither, Cam vowed. Damned if he'd let Beth see that she could still turn him inside out.

She sauntered toward him and he admired that slow, perfect walk. She'd always had a way of moving that made a man think of silk sheets and moonlight.

"Hello, Cam," she said, and that deep, throaty voice of hers fell over him like warm water.

"Beth." He kept his gaze on hers and saw the flash of...*something* there.

"I heard you were moving back."

"Hard to keep secrets in Royal," he said. Just as it was hard to read her expression. Her eyes were shimmering—but with what? Memory? Desire? Irritation? Hell, if he knew.

"Were you trying to keep it a secret?"

"No," he replied. "Why would I?"

"No reason, but for the fact you've been back a week and this is the first time you've been in town."

His mouth quirked. "Keeping tabs on me?"

"Hardly." She shook her head, sending that golden hair of hers into a brief, soft swing. Then she lifted one bare shoulder in a shrug that had the bodice of her dress strain against her perfect breasts. "You said it yourself. Hard to keep a secret here. So have you been hiding out at the ranch?"

"Hiding from what?"

She tipped her head to one side and studied him. "Interesting question."

He knew damn well she thought he'd been avoiding her. And, honestly, he wasn't so sure she was wrong. But the point was that she should be on the defensive here, Cam reminded himself. Yet somehow, she'd turned things around until he felt as if he should be explaining himself to her. Well, the hell with that.

"Yeah, I don't hide. Never did. I don't care what other people have to say," he pointed out. "Unlike some."

Anger zipped across her eyes, and he silently congratulated himself on scoring a point. Weirdly, he realized that not only had his attraction to her remained sure and strong, but a streak of bitterness filled him, as well. Fifteen years hadn't been enough to take the sting out of her betrayal.

"That was a long time ago," she said quietly, obviously aware of their rapt audience.

"Doesn't feel so long." Hell, she still wore the same scent. Flowers and mist and the scent of a rain-drenched day that reached out to grab him by the throat and hold on. He really hated that.

Her gaze narrowed. "It does to me."

For a heartbeat or two, their gazes locked and the tension arcing between them was almost a living thing. Cam felt it. He knew she did, too, though she'd never admit it. Memories rushed into his mind. Nights wrapped together in the back of his truck. Plans for a future that would never happen. And, finally, the last conversation they'd had all those years ago.

That memory dropped ice chips into his heart that were almost enough to quench the blistering heat he felt at simply being near her.

Beth broke first. She tore her gaze from his, glanced at a slim gold watch on her left wrist, and then looked at him again. This time her green eyes were blank, reflecting nothing of what she was feeling. Cam wondered idly when she'd learned to do that.

"I'm sorry," she said. "I have an appointment. But of course, welcome home, Cam."

Her welcome was as cool as her tone. He turned to watch her go, his gaze dropping to the curve of her butt and the nearly hypnotic way it swayed with every step. His body stirred, and silently Cam cursed the fact that Beth Wingate could still turn him into a drooling fool.

But he was older now. Wiser, too, by a long shot. There was no way in hell he would allow Beth to tear his future apart as she had his past.

Beth couldn't stop shaking.

For the last week, since she'd heard he was back in Royal, she'd been preparing herself to see Cam Guthrie again. And all of that preparation had gone right out the window the minute his eyes had met hers. Sitting there at the bank president's desk, she would have sworn she'd felt the temperature in the room rise a few degrees, just from Cam's presence. She'd felt his gaze on her as strongly as she would have a touch, and the instant she'd seen him her heartbeat had jumped into a wild gallop.

His dark brown eyes were filled with shadows. His black hair was cut shorter than she remembered, and he wore a well-tailored suit as easily as he had worn jeans and scuffed boots back when he was the center of her world.

Beth took a deep breath and tried to steady herself. It should have been easy. More than a decade since she'd laid eyes on Cam should have meant that seeing him would be like running into an old friend.

But she'd been fooling herself. Cam hadn't been her friend. He'd been *everything.* Until that last night. When she'd discovered that what a man said and what he did were sometimes two different things.

Now he was home and she'd be dealing with him all the time. How was this fair? Why hadn't he stayed in California? Then she thought that maybe his wife's death had been enough to drive him from the state that was no doubt filled with memories of the two of them together. Had he missed Julie so much? Had he loved her more than he'd ever loved Beth? Because he'd come back to Texas, where he had to face *her* every day and that apparently didn't bother him.

God, she had a headache. Rubbing at the spot between her eyes, Beth reminded herself that nothing had to change because he was here in Royal. There was nothing between them but for the bittersweet memories they shared of being too young and reckless to realize that love wasn't always enough.

"Fifteen years, Beth. Neither of you are the same

people you used to be." Wise words. Now all she had to do was listen to her own good advice.

The early summer sun blasted down on her until she felt as though she was about to combust. Internally, fires were burning while, externally, the Texas heat was only making things worse. She stopped under a bright blue-and-green awning stretched over the florist shop window and hoped the shade would help lower her body temperature.

"It would take more than that," she muttered, and shot a quick glance around to make sure no one had overheard her.

On the busy Main Street, she was alone and she wondered how everyone in town could be going on about their business as if the world hadn't just shifted. Cam was back. He was gorgeous. And treacherous. Sexy. And faithless.

Looking into his eyes had cost her every ounce of self-control she'd worked so hard to develop.

"Hi, Beth!"

She jolted, looked up and nodded at Vonnie Taylor as she pushed her twins past in a double stroller. Beth ignored a twinge of envy as she watched the woman hurry down the sidewalk and reminded herself that she had a rich, full life and she didn't need a man or children to fulfill her. It was true of course, but a part of her still yearned.

Not for Cam, though. That was over and done a long time ago. A few stray thermonuclear hormone reactions notwithstanding, she was fine on her own. Hadn't she just a month ago told Justin McCoy that she wasn't interested in a relationship? Not that the man listened at all. They'd been dating for months and Justin was pushing for more of a commitment. Which was exactly why she'd told him they should take a break from each other.

Having zero men in her life had to be less complicated than what she was dealing with now. With that thought firmly in mind, she started walking again and didn't stop until she came to the Royal Diner. She stepped inside and a wave of air-conditioned air slid across her skin. Grateful, she sighed a little, looked around the room and spotted her friend and assistant, Gracie Diaz. Thankful to get her life back to normal, Beth smiled and headed toward the booth in the back.

The Royal Diner hadn't changed in decades. Well, that wasn't quite true. There had been updates of course, but when the work was done, the color scheme and feel of the place remained the same. Black-and-white checkerboard-tiled floor, red faux-leather booths and even a working juke box on one wall.

Sooner or later, everyone in Royal stopped in at the diner, and so naturally it was the gossip hub. Anything you wanted to know, you could discover here. She couldn't help wondering how long it would be before she and Cam were the latest hot topic of conversation.

She waved to Amanda Battles, who owned the diner along with her sister, Pam.

When Beth was halfway to her booth, Pam called out, "Hi, Beth! The usual?"

"Yes, thanks. You're a lifesaver." She slid into the seat opposite Gracie and set her cream-colored bag beside her on the bench seat.

"Rough morning?" Gracie quipped and smiled.

"You have no idea." A wry smile curved her mouth briefly. She really needed this time with a friend. To cool down. To regain some sort of stability after that quick, devastating encounter with Cam.

Looking across the table at Gracie, Beth saw warm brown eyes, long, straight dark hair that fell, as Beth's did, straight down her back. She wore a pale yellow sleeveless summer blouse and khaki slacks with a pair of sandals that Beth had coveted since the first time she had seen them.

Gracie had grown up on the Wingate ranch, since her parents had worked for Beth's parents. As kids, they'd played and run wild on the ranch. In school, they hadn't really hung out because Beth was three years older than Gracie. But at the ranch, they'd been close and supported each other through the inevitable crushes on boys. And when Gracie had graduated from college, Beth had hired her as an administrative assistant. Best move she'd ever made, since Gracie was as organized as Beth, and together they kept the many different charities Beth managed straight and growing.

Gracie studied her for a long minute, then said, "Okay, something is really going on. Tell me."

Beth waited as Pam served her the usual. A club sandwich and a tall glass of unsweetened black ice tea. "Thanks, Pam."

"You bet." She turned to Gracie. "Can I get you another soda?"

"No, thanks. I'm good." To prove it, she took a sip, then idly picked up one of the french fries that accompanied her burger.

"Okay then," Pam said. She looked at both women and added, "Need anything, just ask."

There was comfort, Beth thought, in the ordinary. In the routine of life in Royal. Of knowing the people in town and realizing that they knew and cared for her, too. So she'd just cling to that mental comfort while she thought about the *discomfort* of seeing Cam.

She took a sip of tea and blurted, "I just ran into Camden at the bank."

Gracie, being the excellent friend she was, didn't need more. "Oh, my God! That had to be awful. Everyone watching…"

"Exactly." That had actually been the hardest part of the whole thing. Beth had felt the curious gazes locked on the pair of them, as if everyone at the bank had been waiting for a big scene. Heck, she'd half expected one herself. The last time she and Cam had *talked*, it hadn't gone well.

"How's he look?" Gracie asked.

"Delicious," Beth muttered.

"Uh-oh."

Beth's gaze shot to her friend's. "Oh, no. No worries there. He's gorgeous and tall and sexy and—" She stopped and took a breath. If she really wanted her hormones to die down, she had to stop thinking about just how good Cam had looked. "It doesn't matter. I made my choice fifteen years ago."

"Uh-huh."

It was Gracie's sarcastic tone more than her words that caught Beth's attention. "I'm sorry? Whose side are you on again?"

"Yours, but," her friend added, "I know bull when I hear it, too."

Like a balloon meeting a sharp pin, Beth simply deflated. Shoulders slumped, she took another sip of her tea and admitted, "Fine. I'm still susceptible to the Guthrie magic."

"There you go. The first step is admitting you have a problem."

Beth laughed shortly. "Is there a Getting Over Cam Guthrie meeting I could attend?"

"You're there already," Gracie said. "I'm here to help you be strong. To avoid all thoughts of sexy

Cam and remember just how badly it all went back in the day."

"Not like I could forget it," Beth mumbled, and picked up a triangle of her sandwich. Taking a bite she didn't really want, she methodically chewed, and as she did, she remembered the last time she'd seen Cam. Back when he was *all* she could see. Back when she believed he loved her. Back before he left town with Julie Wheeler, never to be seen again.

Her heart thudded in her chest, and what felt like an ice-cold stone dropped into the pit of her stomach.

"There you go." Gracie gave her a smile. "Cam was the past, and now you have Justin."

Oh, she didn't want to get into Justin McCoy right now. That was over, too, though he hadn't accepted the fact yet.

Deliberately she took another bite of her sandwich, chewed and said, "Enough about my pitiful love life. Did you track down the caterer for the Fire Department Open House?"

"I did." Accepting the change of subject, Gracie dug into her black oversize leather bag and pulled out a manila folder. "Turns out she's been in Galveston for a family thing."

"That's nice," Beth murmured. "But she's on track and we're covered for the event this Saturday?"

"Oh, absolutely. She's emailed me the finished menu for your final approval. I've got it right here." Gracie handed over a single sheet of paper, and while

Beth looked it over, she continued. "She says they'll be there by ten a.m. to start the setup."

"Okay, that should work." She handed back the paper. "The menu looks great. Finger food, easy to carry around so people can talk and walk or sit down if they want to."

"I'll let her know."

Beth nodded. "The open house at the fire station starts at one, and I want to hold the raffle by three. Give us time to get as many people there as possible."

"It's a brilliant idea, Beth." Gracie shook her head in admiration. "Getting Connolly motors to donate a new truck for the raffle? A nice write-off for them, and raffling it off to raise money for the firehouse is really going well."

Beth thought about that for a minute and acknowledged that her assistant was right. By the time the raffle was done, the Royal Fire Department would have enough money to renovate the old station and buy new equipment without dinging the town for it.

With the catering, the live country music band she'd hired and the guided tours of the firehouse, Beth knew that most of the town would turn out for the event. All of them would be hoping to win that shiny red truck.

"Well, now that we've got that one figured out, let's talk about the food drive for the local shelter."

"Great." Gracie dipped her head, and her long, dark brown hair fell across her shoulders. "We've put up signs at the schools, asking kids to bring in canned or boxed food. Granted, it's the end of the school year, so that won't last long. Still, it's going great, so far. Plus, the grocery store is pitching in, running a special on canned foods. They've set up donation boxes at both entrances, trying to make it easy for people to pitch in."

"Perfect. It's only June," Beth said, opening up her phone and checking through the lists on her notepad. "I want to make sure everyone's fully stocked long before winter."

"You bet. I've got Tucker Davis hauling the donations to our storage units." She glanced up. "The drive ends next Friday, and Tucker said he and his brothers can deliver all of it to the shelter, so we don't have to hire a separate company."

"Awesome." She made a quick note, reminding herself to call Tucker herself and thank him for his help.

While Gracie went through the inventory, Beth's mind wandered. Naturally, it took a sharp turn back to Cam Guthrie. He'd been such a huge part of her life, and then he was gone.

He'd unexpectedly married Julie Wheeler, a girl from their class, and the "happy" couple had left Royal—all within a month of Beth refusing to marry him.

He'd turned to Julie so heartbreakingly fast it had forced Beth to admit that Cam had never really loved her. It had all been a lie, and she was lucky that she'd had the sense to end it before she'd married the man.

Lucky, she reminded herself.

She was alone.

And lucky.

Two

Beth was beginning to feel depressed and wasn't going to put up with it. "You know what, Gracie?" she said suddenly, "Let's eat our lunch and let the rest go for today."

Surprise flashed in the other woman's eyes. "What about the masquerade charity ball at the TCC?"

Beth frowned a little and nibbled at a french fry. That was a big one. They'd be raising money for the children's wing of the local hospital. So that ball had to come off perfectly. She smiled to herself. There was nothing to worry about. It was months away and they were both on top of the situation.

"It'll be perfect, Gracie, because you and I will make sure of it. But we don't have to do it today. The ball's not until October, so we've got a little wiggle room. Enough, at least, for us to enjoy the rest of the day anyway."

"You convinced me," Gracie said, smiling. She picked up her hamburger and took a bite.

"That was easy." Beth laughed, too, and bit into her own sandwich. When she'd swallowed, she asked, "So, did you get your Powerball ticket?"

Gracie grinned. "You bet. My mom always said if you don't play, you can't win. So I buy my ticket once a month, just like she always did—until she decided to save her money instead." Laughing a little, she added, "If I win, I'm going to buy Mom a big house in Florida near her sister, and then I'm going to start up that event planning business I've always wanted."

Beth sipped at her tea. "You know, I'm still willing to back you in that. If you won't take money as a gift, we could call it a loan. Just enough to get you started."

Gracie shook her head firmly. "Nope. Thank you though, Beth. I appreciate it. But I'm saving my money, and when I have enough, I'll apply for a small business loan. I need to do it on my own. But once I'm open I may be ready for investors..." She grinned at that. "And maybe I'll win the lottery!"

"God, you're stubborn." Beth laughed and picked up her sandwich again.

"That's why we get along so well," Gracie told her. "We have so much in common."

Wryly she said, "Good point."

For the next half hour, Beth didn't think about Cam and what him being back in town might cost her.

Cam was still reeling from bumping into Beth at the bank. Hell, it had been ages since he'd seen her. He for damn sure hadn't expected his body's instant response to her, and there was no denying it, either. One look into her eyes, and he was back in the past, on hot summer nights, in the bed of his truck, lying on a blanket, tangled up with a naked Beth.

For years, he'd pushed those memories into a deep, dark hole in his mind. He had been married to Julie after all, and she was the one who had deserved his loyalty. They'd had a good marriage, he told himself. Together, they'd built a house-flipping business that had made them more money than either of them had dreamed possible. They'd been happy. Until Julie got sick. Then it had been doctors and hospitals and a fast slide to the end. In a matter of months, Cam had lost her and any interest he might have had to keep their business going.

But with her gone, there was nothing to hold him in California, and the pull of his roots was too strong to fight.

Now he was back and he'd bought the ranch he and his parents had once worked on. The Circle K… "Have to change that," he muttered, stepping out of his truck to stand and take a good look around.

The sun was hotter now, beating down on him until he thought that maybe Texas was planning on giving him a baptism of fire as a welcome home. The air was still, not a hint of wind to rustle the live oaks surrounding the ranch house.

He turned to look at the place and felt a stir of pride. Buying this ranch was satisfying in a way Cam hadn't really expected. It was as if coming back to Royal was returning to Texas, but owning this place was coming *home.*

He'd only been back in town for a week, but this house… It was as if it had been waiting for him all these years. It needed fixing up, definitely some updates. The kitchen alone made him cringe and ready to grab a sledgehammer. And he had plans for expansion, too. Some of it he'd do himself, because fifteen years of being both entrepreneur and carpenter was hard to shake. But for most of what he wanted done, he'd already hired Olivia Turner and her construction company.

He leaned back against his brand-new gleaming black truck and took it all in. Two stories, the house was built of river stone, boasted a red tile roof, and its design successfully mixed Spanish and craftsman styles. There was a wide balcony around the second floor of the house and a wraparound porch on the ground floor.

The view from the front was a wide sweep of ranchland, the corral and, off to the side, a barn that was painted the rich, dark green of young meadow grass. There were outbuildings for the ranch hands, a bunkhouse and a separate house for the foreman, Henry Jordan and his family.

Cam's plans to turn this place into a sort of working dude ranch meant that he'd need Olivia's company to build a dozen cottages for guests and another stable for the extra horses he was going to have to buy. Which meant, he told himself, they'd also require more ranch hands, but he'd leave the hiring to Henry. He'd be working with them and knew practically every cowboy in Texas, so there was no point in Cam sticking his nose in. He was a big believer in delegating. Find the best person for the job and then get out of their way.

One day, Cam would think about making the house bigger because he wanted a family, eventually. He and Julie had tried, but things hadn't worked out.

When his cell phone rang, Cam reached for it gratefully. He was willing to thank whoever it was taking him out of his own head for a while. He glanced at the screen, smiled and answered.

"Hi, Darren."

"Hey, do you miss us yet?"

Cam laughed a little. Darren Casey was his partner in a home improvement line of products they'd started up four years ago. Darren had the manufacturing experience and Cam had his name and the fame he'd built as a house flipper.

He hadn't been looking to be famous, just to make a good living. But, as word had spread about Cam and Julie's gift for rehabbing houses, they'd earned sponsors, clients and, finally, their own show for two years on a home and garden network. Then Julie had gotten sick and…

Shrugging out of his suit jacket, he loosened his tie, undid the collar button on his shirt and wished desperately for the gray Stetson he'd left in the house that morning. He undid the cuffs on his shirt and rolled the sleeves up to his elbows.

"That depends," he answered, only half joking, "what's the weather in Huntington Beach like?"

Darren laughed. "Same as every year at this time. About sixty-five and cloudy."

Right now, Cam thought with a glance at the cloudless, brassy sky, the June Gloom of Southern California sounded great.

"Are you frying in Texas already?"

Damned if he'd admit to that with it only being June, so Cam changed the subject. "You call to talk about the weather?"

"Not really. We got an offer to expand our line of tools into the biggest home improvement hardware outlet in the country."

"Yeah?" He grinned and leaned back against the truck. They were already in a nationwide department store, but this offer would seriously put their tools into the hands of do-it-yourselfers across the country.

"Tell me the details." While the other man talked, Cam let his gaze wander across the house, the land and the future he planned to build there.

Beth used to love this house, he remembered. They had talked about buying it one day, raising a family here. But that was when they were kids and the future looked big and bright and the only problem he had was keeping his hands off her whenever they were together.

Back then, Cam had had no money but lots of dreams. Now he had enough money for ten men, but no dreams.

He'd come home to change that.

So much for taking the day off.

Beth hadn't been able to stand it. If she was going to be seeing Cam on a regular basis, then she wanted to lay down some ground rules. She'd practically run from him at the bank and that really bothered her. Why should *she* run? He should have turned around the moment he'd seen her. But, no. Cam Guthrie did what he wanted, when he wanted. Always had.

Well, she promised herself, until now.

Which was why when they'd finished lunch, she'd left Gracie in town and steered her car toward Cam's new ranch. If her stomach was dipping and rolling at the prospect of being near him again, she ignored it. Eventually she'd get used to having him in town, right? All she had to do was get past the first rush of whatever was driving her crazy.

The road stretched out in front of her, and Beth realized she could have driven to him in her sleep. She knew every dip, every curve and every damn oak lining the road. Just as she'd once known Cam—or thought she had, anyway.

"Doesn't matter," she muttered. "The past is gone, this is now."

Even as she thought about it, that past roared into life in her mind. The images tumbling through her brain were so vivid, so real, she had to shake her head to dislodge them or risk driving her car right into a tree. It didn't matter that she could remember how Cam had smiled at her. How he would swoop in to kiss her and lift her off her feet as he turned her in a slow circle while their mouths fused. Didn't matter that he'd left her because of one fight.

That he'd turned to Julie overnight and married her as if Beth hadn't meant a thing to him after all. How much time had she wasted wondering if there'd been signs all along that he didn't really love her? Had he been cheating on her with Julie behind her back? She wanted to know—and she didn't. Just like she didn't want to revisit her old relationship with everyone she bumped into just because Cam was back in town.

He'd been gone a long time and she'd been here. Building her life. Her reputation. She wasn't going to risk any of it just because Camden Guthrie had decided to return to Royal.

She punched the accelerator and was suddenly glad she'd left the top down on her bright scarlet BMW. Yes, her hair would look like hell when she got to Cam's place, but hopefully, the rushing wind would push all memories out of her mind.

No such luck.

Because as she made a left into the wide drive, those memories flooded into her consciousness whether she wanted them or not.

Oaks still lined the drive, though of course they were bigger now. Flowers grew wild and tangled in the once tidy beds, and the drive itself needed to be regraveled. But the house at the end of the drive was as she remembered it, if in need of some fresh paint on the storm shutters and the front porch. Beth had always loved this place, but now she wondered if it was only because Cam had lived here.

"Doesn't matter," she assured herself.

His truck was parked out front. As she tore up the drive, Cam opened the front door and moved to the edge of the porch to watch her approach. Her heart did that frantic, racing beat again, and as much as she fought it, Beth was half-afraid this would always be her reaction to him. But that didn't mean she had to act on it.

"For God's sake, *remember* that," she muttered as she threw her car into Park and turned off the engine. Quickly Beth ran both hands through her hair, then opened the door and stepped out. The air was breathless—or maybe that was just her.

She looked up at him. "Hello, Cam."

He nodded. "Beth. Didn't expect to see you here," he said.

"Yes, well," she answered honestly, "I didn't expect me here, either."

He laughed shortly and took the six wide steps down to the drive. She'd always loved watching him walk. It was definitely a cowboy amble, a slow, deliberate stride that made a woman think that he did *everything* that slowly. And Beth was here to testify that he certainly did. At least some of the time. He could also be fast and explosive. Either way, she admitted silently, was memorable.

Cam had traded his expensive suit for a black T-shirt that clung to his broad chest and a pair of jeans that hugged his long legs and stacked on the toes of his black boots.

Danger! Danger! She heard the warning shriek in her mind, but she was here now and it was too late to walk away without looking exactly like the coward she would be if she left.

"What can I do for you, Beth?"

Oh, there was a loaded question. She could think of so many things he could do for her. And that was not what she should be thinking.

She inhaled sharply, gave herself a silent, stern

warning and said, “Cam, I thought we should talk, now that you’re back home.”

He came closer, stopped a foot from her, leaned against his truck and folded his arms over his chest. “Talk about what?”

“Seriously?” Beth stared at him for a long second or two. “You can ask me that?”

“What’s got you so worried, Beth? Me? Or *you*?”

A little of both, but he didn’t need to know that. “Please. I’m not a love-blinded teenager anymore, Cam. I’m not here to throw myself at your feet.”

“Good to know.” He pushed one hand through his hair. “Fine. You want to talk? Let’s talk about why we have to dredge up the past.”

“Oh, we don’t,” she assured him. “I’m here to talk about what happens now that you’re back.”

“Uh-huh.”

“Look,” she continued, since he was just staring at her. Damn it. “I just think we need to have some ground rules. So we both know where we stand.”

“Is that right?” He straightened up, and one corner of his mouth quirked. “And I suppose you get to decide what the rules are?”

“You bet I do,” she countered quickly. “I’m the one who’s been here. You left.”

All semblance of a smile left his face. “And you know why.”

She blinked at him, stunned. Did he honestly believe that? “No, Camden. Actually, I don’t know.

And fifteen years later, I don't want to know. What I want is to not be gossiped about. Again."

"Bull." One word. Clipped. Angry. "You know what the hell happened as well as I do. As for not wanting to be gossiped about? Can't avoid that, Beth. Gossip is the blood of Royal."

"Don't tell me about the town you haven't set foot in over a decade."

"I grew up here, too. Far as I can tell, nothing much has changed."

He had a point, but that didn't mean she had to admit it. She spun around, took two steps, then turned back to face him. "This is my home, Camden."

"Mine, too," he said tightly. "I'm here and I'm not leaving. You're going to have to get used to it. I know you prefer having everything run the way you arrange it, but some things are just out of your control."

Again. Stunned. "Maybe I do have a little bit of a control issue, but let's remember who it was who had our whole *lives* planned out. That was you, Cam."

"Yeah. Worked out great, didn't it?"

Beth felt as if the top of her head might just blow off. She deliberately took several deep breaths and reminded herself how far she'd come from the girl she'd been so long ago. She didn't owe Cam anything, but she owed herself plenty.

"I didn't come out here to fight," she said calmly.

"And yet..."

She gritted her teeth. "We have to come to an arrangement." Cam was insisting he was home to stay, but she wasn't sure she believed him. He'd been in California for so long, why wouldn't he get tired of ranching life and run right back to the beaches?

Off in the distance, Beth heard the whinny of horses and a couple of the working cowboys shouting to each other. The wind was still, the sun was blasting down on them, and Camden's brown eyes were filled with shifting shadows.

"What do you have in mind?" he asked.

She lifted her chin, met his gaze and stiffly said, "We keep our distance from each other for one."

"Not a problem."

That was easy. A little insulting, but easy. She remembered a time when spending one day away from each other had been like a short visit to hell.

As if he could read her thoughts, his mouth curved again. "What's the matter, Beth? Afraid you can't keep your hands off me?"

She gritted her teeth again. Why had she once found him so irresistible? "I think I can manage."

"We'll see, won't we?"

"Then you agree?" she asked.

"Not yet."

"What?" She hadn't expected that. They'd been apart forever. She hadn't seen him in years. He'd been *married* to someone else, for God's sake. Why would he have a problem with the two of them avoiding each other? "Why not?"

He looked down into her eyes and drawled, "Did you really think I'd just roll over and do whatever you told me to do?"

Yes, damn it. "Of course not. I'm just trying to make this easier on both of us."

"Ah." He nodded. "So thoughtful. Well, thanks for your concern, but I can take care of myself."

"So you won't agree?"

"I didn't say that."

Irritation fired up inside Beth until she wanted to tear at her hair. "What *are* you saying then?"

"Simple. You have a plan. I'll go along, but I want something in return."

Outraged, she sucked in a gulp of air. "You're really going to ask *me* for a favor? You're going to *bargain* with me? After what you did?"

He held up one hand. "Nope, not talking about the past, remember?"

Beth fought the urge to climb back into her car and drive away, leaving him in a cloud of dust. The only thing keeping her there was the knowledge that she had to get him to agree to a truce or Royal wasn't going to be big enough for both of them.

"And it's not a favor," Cam said. "Let's call it quid pro quo."

Folding her arms across her middle, Beth tipped her head to one side and met his gaze steadily. She should have known Camden wouldn't go along with her plan. He'd always been stubborn. Always wanted things his own way. Of course, so had she. Which was just one of the reasons that their relationship had been filled with fire, excitement, passion… She shook her head. "Fine. What do you want?"

Squinting, he said, "Getting hotter out here. You want to come in and get out of the sun?"

She shot a quick glance at the house, then looked back at him. Alone in the house with him? Hoo, boy. That was too much of a temptation. "No. Just tell me, Cam."

"Fine. I want to join the TCC."

That's what he wanted? Seriously? She'd thought that maybe he wanted to call a truce between them. Or donate a kidney to some deserving soul. Or hell, paint his house neon yellow. But the TCC?

Throwing up her hands, she demanded, "Well, who's stopping you?"

He scrubbed one hand across the back of his neck. "No one that I know of," he admitted. "Yet. Burt Wheeler's the treasurer though and he's not one of my biggest fans. He won't do me any good when my application comes before the membership committee."

Burt Wheeler. Camden's father-in-law, who still blamed Camden for taking Julie away from Royal. He'd never really gotten over his daughter moving away to California, and when she died, it had nearly killed Burt. Beth could understand why there might be bad blood between Cam and the older man.

"Fine. What do you expect me to do about it?"

"Use your influence." He shoved both hands into his back pockets. "Hell, Beth, you're a Wingate. Your family has always ruled this town. You speak up for me to the president— Who is president of the TCC now?"

"James Harris." Two years older than Camden, the two men hadn't been friends growing up, but it was impossible to grow up in Royal and not know everyone.

"Good. He's a fair man." Cam nodded. "If a Wingate speaks to James for me, it'll go a long way."

He wasn't wrong, Beth acknowledged. The Wingate name carried a lot of weight in Royal and in many other places, as well. She used that name to foster the charities she supported and ran. So supporting Cam at the club would be an easy enough thing to do. But, first, she had to know what was driving him.

"Why is this so important to you? You never used to care about the Texas Cattleman's Club." Had he really changed so much? "Heck, you used to make fun of the old guard gathering at their own private 'watering hole.' Now you want in?"

"I'm opening a business and I want that support behind me when I do." He pulled his hands free, slapped one palm on the hood of his truck and instantly lifted it off again with a hiss of pain. "Damn thing's hot. Anyway, everyone knows you need the TCC stamp of approval if you want a business in Royal to succeed."

A business. She wondered why he would bother. Beth knew darn well that he was already sitting on a fortune. Why not just be a rich cowboy and enjoy what he'd already built. What did he have to prove? He'd been on *television* for heaven's sake. Huh. Was that what he was up to?

"You fixing to flip houses here like you did in California? Want to film a new handyman show? Because you won't find that many run-down neighborhoods in Royal."

"No." He shook his head. "I'm done with all of that."

She waited, but he didn't offer any more information and Beth didn't ask. She wanted to, but damned if she'd give him the satisfaction of knowing she was curious. Was he finished with the flipping business because Julie was gone now and he couldn't bear to do it without her? Had he loved his wife that much? Were memories of Julie haunting him? A twinge of pain ached in her heart. Beth pushed it aside, though she couldn't stop the questions rushing through her mind. Still, she kept quiet.

"Fine," she said finally. "I'll do what I can for you at the TCC on one condition."

His brown eyes narrowed on her. "You already

laid down your condition. We don't talk. We avoid each other. Remember?"

"Yeah, but now that's not enough." She had him and they both knew it. He needed her and she wasn't going to waste this opportunity.

Wary now, he asked, "What do you want?"

"A very hefty donation to my favorite charity."

Both eyebrows rose. She'd surprised him. Well, good. Maybe that would convince him that he didn't know her as well as he thought he did. They'd both changed a lot over the years.

"We're going to build a new children's wing at Royal hospital and I'm in charge of raising the money." She smoothed the skirt of her dress. "I'm fund-raising now, and I think a donation from you will go a long way toward convincing the TCC membership that you're the kind of man they want as a member."

His eyes narrowed on her suspiciously. "Sounds like blackmail to me."

"That's an ugly word." She examined her fingernails and made a mental note to get a manicure tomorrow. "I prefer the term *extortion*."

He snorted.

"There's going to be a big charity ball at the TCC in October to raise money for the new wing," she said, catching his eye. "And if you make a *substantial* donation, I'll make sure you're a member before then."

He took a deep breath and let it out again. “Hell, you’ve got more of your father in you than I ever noticed.”

Beth knew he meant that as an insult. Her father hadn’t liked Cam at all back in the day. Cam, of course, had decided it was because his mother had been a Tigua Indian.

Trent hadn’t cared about that, though Beth had never been able to convince Cam of it. Her father’s resistance had come from the fact that he hadn’t wanted his daughter falling in love with a simple ranch hand. She was a Wingate. That meant she had a duty to marry someone as rich as they were. To continue the dynasty.

Beth had ignored her father’s plans for her because, back then, all she’d been able to see was Cam. And, she told herself, look where that had gotten her. Thankfully now, her eyes were wide open.

“If you mean that, like my father, I know how to get things done, then yes. You’re absolutely right.”

He snorted again.

“That’s so rude.”

Cam grinned. “I know. Okay, we have a deal.”

“The whole thing,” she qualified. “The donation, the staying away from each other…”

“And the membership in the TCC,” he put in.

“Agreed.” She held out one hand and his right hand enveloped hers.

Three

Instantly, Beth knew she'd made a mistake in touching him. Heat erupted, shooting up her arm to her chest, where it settled and burned with an intensity she hadn't known in fifteen years. Shaking hands with Cam had obviously been a bad idea—yet she couldn't regret feeling that burn again.

She'd been with other men since they had broken up, of course. Most recently, Justin McCoy. But it was only Cam who could make her feel like this. Only Cam who could make her blood sizzle with a look. Make her yearn with a mere touch.

When she tried to pull away, he tightened his grip, holding on to her hand as he locked his gaze with hers. Electricity seemed to dart back and forth between them, forging a link that blistered and burned.

"Stay away from each other?" he asked, and his voice was so deep it rumbled in the still air.

She swallowed hard. "Yes. Definitely, yes."

He let her go and she curled her fingers into her palm in a futile attempt to somehow keep that heat close.

"All right." He nodded. "We'll do it your way. Again."

Well, *that* had her head snapping up and her eyes firing into his. The fresh memory of heat and hunger disappeared in the rush of fury. "Again? What are you saying? Somehow this is all *my* fault?"

"You're the one who broke up with me, remember? Who the hell else's fault could it be?"

Beth laughed as she stared at him, dumbfounded. "I didn't break up with you. That's only what you heard. All I said was we had to slow down."

"Right." Cam snorted. "Slow down. Female code for 'see ya.'"

Stunned, she gaped at him. "Wow. That is so sexist."

"I'm not a sexist."

"So you just say stupid things."

"Not stupid, either," Cam retorted, his gaze drilling into hers.

"And I don't speak in code."

He laughed shortly again and she thought the

sound was so damn annoying it grated on her every nerve.

"All women speak in code."

"Just because men don't understand anything that doesn't begin with their zippers..."

"Ah, sure"

"And lumping me in with my entire gender is insulting."

"Too bad. You just lumped me in with mine." Shaking his head slowly, he kept his gaze fixed on hers. "You might not like the memory, Beth, but that doesn't change a damn thing. You were the one who set this all in motion. Just you."

"No, you don't." She took a step closer and kept her gaze fixed on his so he wouldn't miss the outrage glimmering in her eyes. "If you want to rewrite history, do it with someone who didn't live it with you. I'm not the one who turned away and married the first person they saw and then left the damn state."

"If that's the way you're looking at it, you're wrong. *You* walked away, Beth," he said tightly. "I just walked *farther* than you did."

Her head snapped back as if she'd been slapped. Did he really look back and see that he was the good guy? The innocent? How long had it taken for him to absolve himself? Until his wedding night with Julie? Is that when Beth had been shoved neatly into a drawer and forgotten about?

Or had it been sooner?

"I can't believe this." Her voice was low, carrying the ring of astonishment. "You're *defending* what you did? Do you know how humiliating it was for me around here? For months after you and Julie left town, people stared at me. Wondering what had happened. Spreading rumors."

She'd never forget it. The sympathetic stares from people or, worse, the amused glances of girls she'd thought were her friends. "My own mother thought I was pregnant and that's why you left. Everywhere I went, whispered conversations stopped when I got close. There were guys who thought they could move right into your place. And my so-called friends turned on me like rabid snakes, gossiping, laughing.

"There was no way to avoid any of it. I was alone because you were *gone.* I finally left for college and it felt like an escape."

He laughed a little under his breath. "Wow. You escaped. Good for you. Do you want a prize? Do you know the crap I heard when my friends found out you'd dumped me?"

"I didn't dump you. *You* dumped *me*. Pretty damn publicly, too. And you didn't have to listen to them for months, did you?" She glared up at him, feeling the fury that had been buried inside her for fifteen years rising up to the surface. "Just how long had you been cheating on me with Julie?"

Clearly shocked, he blurted, *"What?"*

"You married Julie like a week after we broke up—"

"So you agree, you broke up with me."

"No, I didn't say that. And don't change the subject. You and Julie got married and skipped town in like ten seconds. And I was left here, trying to explain how my boyfriend of three years had married someone else!"

His brown eyes turned thunderous and a part of Beth was happy to see it. Why should she be the only one upset?

"I don't owe you an explanation, Beth," he ground out.

"Yeah, you do. But I'll never get one." She whirled away, took a step and looked back. "You go ahead and tell yourself whatever lie you have to, to make yourself feel better. I know the truth. And whether you admit it or not, so do you."

He was after her in a heartbeat. She shouldn't have been surprised, but she was. She'd forgotten how fast he could move. Beth gasped as he took her arm, spun her around and then held on to her shoulders. He was looming over her and he did it well. He was so tall she had to tip her head back to meet brown eyes that were flashing with indignation.

"You think it was easy for me?" he demanded.

"Yes," she snapped. "You're damn right I do. You and Julie got out. Just the two of you. It's more than I had."

"You're wrong," he said. "Nothing about leaving here was easy."

She hoped not. "I don't care."

"Yeah, you made that clear the last night we were together."

He kept trying to make her feel guilty about that night. But she'd done nothing wrong. She couldn't regret it even now. She'd been right to go with her gut. With her heart. It hadn't meant she didn't love Cam. It felt as if she'd *always* loved him. And a part of her still did. Naturally, she kept *that* part locked away in a corner of her mind she never explored.

"I was only eighteen, Cam."

"And I was nineteen," he reminded her. "What's your point?"

"My point is, I did what I had to. You didn't see how young I was—how young we were—back then, and you still don't."

"I saw it," he argued. "I didn't care. Didn't think it mattered. We had a plan, Beth. And you scrapped it without a thought. Well, I did what I had to do, too. I found a way to survive what *you* did to me."

She laughed again and the sound was painful, even to her. "Marrying Julie was a survival technique? Well, hell, Cam. You should teach a course on that at the city college. *How to Get Over Heartbreak by Marrying Someone Else.* I'm sure tons of men would sign up for that one."

"That's not what I meant."

"It's what you said."

"Damn it, Beth." He shook his head, stared up at the sky for a slow count of five, then looked back at her. "You always had the hardest head."

She inhaled sharply and held up one hand. "Don't. You don't get to pretend you still know me. I'm not that young girl anymore. We're not together now and we're never going to be."

"Who said I wanted us back together?"

His words stung in spite of what she was feeling. She wouldn't let him see the hurt, though. "Good, then we're on the same page."

"Almost."

She huffed out a breath. "What's that supposed to mean?"

"Well, hell, if we're going to avoid each other and we're never going to be together again, then we need to do something we *didn't* do fifteen years ago."

Actually, Beth couldn't think of a single thing they hadn't done back then. And remembering everything they *had* done made her heartbeat skip and her blood hum through her veins. It seemed fury wasn't enough to squash the kind of desire that pumped through her whenever Cam was near. "What's that?"

His gaze fixed on hers, one corner of his mouth lifted into a tiny, secretive smile that used to drive her crazy with need. "Well," he said softly, "we never did kiss goodbye."

And he swooped in on her just like he used to.

She'd pushed him, just as she used to. Made him feel too much, just as she used to. And just like when they were kids, Cam swept Beth off her feet and pressed her tightly to his chest. Then he fused his mouth to hers as if she held his next breath. And while he fed a need that had haunted him for years, one corner of his mind was alert to her reaction.

Would she push him away? Would she tear her mouth free and shout "no"? It would kill him to stop, but damned if he'd hold her if she didn't want him to.

But she hooked her arms around his neck almost instantly and everything in him roared into life.

The taste of her filled him. Her scent seemed to surround him, drawing him in, drawing him back to a time when she was everything to him.

But memories paled when compared to having her back in his arms again. She parted her lips and at the first slide of his tongue against hers, Cam was electrified. His body turned to stone, and all he could think was *more.* He held her tighter, pressing her body to his so that she had no doubt of what she was doing to him. His hands swept up and down her spine, and every time she shivered, he felt the fires inside erupt.

Years fell away. Old aches, hurts and regrets faded into the rush of heat that swamped him. All he wanted was to carry her inside to his bedroom, stretch her out across the mattress and bury himself inside her. He craved that connection as he did his next breath.

And that was enough to have Cam breaking the kiss, setting her on her feet and taking a single step back from her. Damned if he'd seduce her on his driveway when a dozen cowboys could glance over at them and get a show.

He looked at Beth as she stared at him while she struggled to catch her breath. He knew how she felt. His own heartbeat was raging, and the ache in his balls made him want to brace his hands on his knees and do some deep breathing until the pain eased.

He hadn't asked for this to happen, though he'd known that coming back to Royal would mean being around Beth again. And maybe pretending it wouldn't happen again really would be lying to himself. What he had to do was remember that she'd betrayed him. Yeah, they were different people now, but how could he trust her, remembering?

Maybe Beth's idea to keep their distance was a good one, but damned if he could see that bargain lasting for long. Royal wasn't big enough for them to avoid each other. But one more episode like this one just might kill him.

"Okay then," she said finally, sounding a little breathless. "You've had your goodbye kiss..."

"Yeah. About that." He locked his gaze with hers. "Didn't really feel like goodbye. It tasted more like *welcome back*."

"No, it didn't." She shook her head as if that action would help.

He grinned in spite of everything. Hell, he remembered Beth arguing even when she was wrong and knew it. In fact, she'd fight back even harder if she was wrong. Like she was now.

"Well, then let's try it again," he challenged, even though another kiss at the moment would bring him to his knees. "See which one of us is right."

She skipped backward a couple steps. "I don't think so. I already know who's right and it's not you."

"Guess we'll see, won't we?" Oh, this wasn't the end of whatever was still simmering between them. Cam knew they were just starting and she knew it, too. Which was why she was inching ever closer to her car.

"Whatever you might be thinking, Camden?" she said, fumbling behind her for the car door handle, "I haven't been standing still waiting for you to come back. You got married. Moved on. Well, so have I."

Surprised, he asked, "Seriously?"

"Is that so hard to believe?" She looked insulted.

"No. But I didn't hear anything about you being married…" And he didn't like thinking about it. Whether it made sense or not didn't matter.

"I'm not," she said. "But I didn't join a convent, either. In fact, there's a man right now who wants to marry me."

"Who?" His guts twisted.

"None of your business. I'm not here for you, Cam. We're not going to hook up again just because we're in the same town now."

His gaze dropped to her left hand. Empty. He

hated that he was relieved to see it. "Well, you're not wearing a ring. So I guess we'll just see what happens, won't we?"

"Nothing's going to happen, Camden."

"Something already did, Beth. Hell, you felt it, too, when we kissed."

She shrugged that off. "It was just a kiss."

"Uh-huh. And a Texas summer is just warm."

She opened the car door and pulled it wide. "I'm not playing this game with you, Cam."

He dropped one hand on the car door and leaned in. "Not a game, Beth."

"Whatever it is, I'm out."

"For now," he said.

"Forever."

He didn't believe that. Not for a damn second. Cam still held on to what she'd said to him their last night together. How she'd walked away from him and everything they'd planned. She'd cut his heart out with a few well-chosen words. But he could also feel the sizzling threads still connecting them. One kiss and he wanted more. And when he had more, he knew it still wouldn't be enough.

Hell, if *he* was willing to set aside the past, she would be, too. She just had to argue about it for a while.

He could wait.

"I'll get you that donation," he said abruptly.

"Right." She nodded, swallowed hard and then

slid into her car, the hem of her dress riding high enough on her thigh to make his mouth go dry. "Once you do that, I'll talk to membership at the TCC and get that ball rolling."

"You're going to wait until you get the money? Don't trust me?"

She looked over her shoulder at him. "Nope."

He laughed. "Fair enough. I don't trust you, either."

Beth put her sunglasses on so he couldn't read her eyes anymore. "Then we know where we stand."

Then she gunned the engine and peeled out of the drive, sending up a wake of dirt and gravel behind her.

The woman always had known how to make an exit.

She wasn't a mile from Cam's ranch when her cell phone rang. Beth glanced at the screen on her dash and sighed. When she answered, she didn't bother to hide the sigh. "What is it, Sutton?"

One of her twin older brothers. Sutton was three minutes younger than Sebastian and way more relaxed and fun than his stoic, dutiful twin. As he constantly reminded everyone, including Sebastian.

"Well, hello to you, too," he said, then asked, "are you driving with the top down? I can hardly hear you."

"Yes, I am and I can hear you fine." Not really. "What is it, Sutton?"

"Why do you bother to answer the phone when you're driving?"

"Why do you *call* me when I'm driving?"

"Because you're always on the move. When else am I going to reach you?"

"Good point." She was always busy. Running the numerous charities that the Wingate Corporation supported was pretty much a 24/7 job. She spent most of her time driving to businesses to wrangle donations or meeting with supporters. "Okay, what's up?"

"Family meeting at the house."

"What?" She steered around a curve in the road, straightened out and demanded, "Why? We just had a meeting two weeks ago. I've got appointments to keep."

"Believe it or not, little sister, we *all* do."

Fine, he had a point. The Wingate family didn't simply sit around and count their money. Their biggest company, WinJet, was huge, having outgrown Texas many years ago. Her brothers, and cousins Luke and Zeke, did most of the heavy lifting there.

"Right. So what's going on?" She barely noticed the scenery flying past as she whipped her beloved BMW convertible down the road. And though she was managing to hold a conversation with Sutton, her mind was still on Camden. Unconsciously, she lifted one hand to her mouth, as if she could still feel his lips on hers. And, really, she could. It was as if he'd branded her.

"Mom called the meeting."

"Mom?" Ever since the death of Beth's father, Ava Wingate had stepped back from the company. She'd gone to Europe for an extended stay, along with one of her oldest "friends," Keith Cooper. How Mom was oblivious to the fact that Keith was clearly in love with her, Beth couldn't figure out. Then again, maybe Ava didn't want to know the truth.

"Did she say what the meeting's about?" Beth asked, concentrating on the road again.

"No. All she said was, attendance is mandatory. Hell, she's even got Piper coming in from Dallas for it."

"Okay, that makes no sense." Her mother's younger sister, Piper Holloway, wasn't even a part of the company.

"Yeah. Look, all I know is Baz called to tell me about the meeting and ordered me to spread the word."

"Ordered?"

He laughed. "You know Baz. He's always ordering everybody around. Part of his charm."

True. Their oldest brother had stepped into the void left behind when their father, Trent, died two years before. Sebastian had a tight grip on the company and under his leadership, Wingate Enterprises, with Win-Jet in the lead, was growing like it never had before.

"Fine," she said, just managing to bury the sigh. "When?"

"Now."

"Damn it!" She pressed harder on the accelerator. "I'm about twenty minutes out. Baz will have to be patient."

"Sure," Sutton said with a laugh. "That'll happen." After a pause, he asked, "Where exactly are you?"

Her mouth worked because she didn't want to say the words, but then told herself she had nothing to be ashamed of. "I'm on Old River Road."

"Huh."

"What?"

"Nothing." Sutton's voice was amused as he added, "Isn't that where Camden Guthrie's ranch is?"

"How do you know that?"

"Everybody knows that. What I don't know is why you went there."

"It's not what you're thinking." Beth winced. She'd known people would start talking about the two of them again.

"How do you know what I'm thinking?"

"Please."

"Fine. I'll leave it alone."

"Thanks." Beth sighed a little.

"For now."

Way too many men were telling her that today.

Family meetings were an unavoidable fact in the Wingate family.

Usually those meetings were at the company

headquarters, but for whatever reason, Ava Wingate had insisted this meeting be held at the family ranch. Boasting forty acres of prime Texas ranch land that had never actually been worked, the Wingates kept horses for personal riding and plenty of chickens for their kitchen needs. The barn and stable were on one side of the property and the guesthouse on the other. The main house sat on the highest point on the property, affording views of untouched rolling hills, a private lake and stands of oaks.

The house itself was sort of a mix of Southwestern and California ranch, made of cream-colored stone and stucco. There was a red clay tile roof, a wide front porch and a wraparound balcony on the second floor.

Beth loved it. She lived at the main house, along with her mom, Sebastian and Sutton. The house was palatial in size, so everyone had privacy and plenty of space. The Wingate cousins, Luke and his twin, Zeke, lived in the guesthouse, so they were close enough to be a part of everything and far enough away that they could get space when they needed it.

Sitting in the formal dining room at a table that could easily seat twenty, Beth glanced around. There were paintings of the ranch dotting the cream-colored walls and the heavy, dark wood beams added interest and a sense of timelessness.

Beth's brothers were on one side of the table while Luke and Zeke sat beside her. Everyone was waiting on Ava and wondering why they were there in the first place.

"The gang's all here," Piper Holloway said brightly as she hurried into the room. She took a seat next to Sebastian and looked around at all of them in turn. Piper was forty, looked thirty and was Ava's younger sister. She was more of a sister to all of them, too, than an aunt. Tall and slim, she kept her dark brown hair in a short, edgy style that looked perfect on her. She owned an art gallery in Dallas, but came home to Royal often. Her dark green eyes were filled with questions as she grinned at Beth.

"Anyone know why we're here yet?"

"No," Beth said. "Mom's running late."

"Was there an apocalypse?" Piper's eyebrows went up. "Ava's never late."

That was true, too. Starting to get worried, Beth leaned into Zeke. "What time is it?"

"Ten minutes past when she said she'd be here."

Beth sighed. She still had to meet with the owners of the local wine store about their donation to the TCC charity masquerade.

"So fill me in," Piper said, looking at all of them. "What's new at the company?"

Sebastian looked at Luke. "You're the VP of New Product Development…"

Luke grinned and leaned both forearms on the shining walnut table. "We've got some interesting drones coming out of R & D."

"Drones?" Beth asked. "They're not new, right?"

"These are." Luke held up one hand, palm out. "They fit in the palm of your hand, and they're so easy to use kids will love them."

Zeke jumped in. "I've got our top guys working on ideas for digital ads as well as commercials already. Luke's drones are awesome."

Zeke and Luke were the sons of Ava's older brother, Robert, the product of his marriage to Nina, an African American woman. When Robert and Nina died in an accident, Ava had insisted that Luke and Zeke come to Royal to be with family. Now it felt as if they'd always been there.

The twins were both tall and gorgeous, with caramel-colored skin, closely cropped black hair and bright green eyes. Zeke was the VP of Marketing while Luke was in charge of New Product Development. The genius of Luke's creative mind was its flexibility, and Zeke's inner adventurer kept everyone on their toes. Beth was nuts about both of them.

Thankfully, they weren't identical, because Sebastian and Sutton were sometimes hard to tell apart. Beth shifted a look at her brothers.

They were tall and handsome, with dark blond hair and the Wingate green eyes. Sebastian was the CEO of Wingate Enterprises, Sutton was the CFO, and Beth was grateful the four guys did the majority of the worrying and working on the family business.

Piper was nudging Sebastian, trying to coax a

smile out of him. Meanwhile, Sutton was kicked back in his chair, grinning at something Zeke had said. Zeke elbowed Luke to bring him in on the joke, and Beth smiled to herself, just watching them.

Sutton and Sebastian were as different as they were identical. Baz was always serious, all business, while Sutton had a ready smile and a relaxed attitude that put everyone at ease.

The only ones missing now, she thought sadly, were her brother Miles and their sister Harley. But Miles had left Royal for Chicago and his own security company years ago and Harley and her son, Daniel, were living in Thailand while she ran her nonprofit, Zest. Beth missed them both. Especially at times like this.

"Anyone know what this is about?" Sutton's question hung in the air.

"You guys would know more about it than I would," Beth said, and looked at Luke.

"Nope. Not a clue," he replied, shaking his head. Then he looked at Sebastian. "Aunt Ava hasn't said anything to you?"

"No." He didn't look happy about that, either. "Ever since Mom came home to work at the company again six months ago, she's been moving around from section to section. Like she's familiarizing herself with everything again."

"It's a good idea," Zeke said.

"The question is," Piper put in, "why did she call us all here?"

"The answer is a simple…yet complex one." Everyone turned to look at Ava as she entered the room.

Everyone came to attention in their seats and Beth had to marvel at it. Ava Holloway Wingate commanded a room once she stepped inside it. Almost sixty, she was the picture of refined elegance. A slight touch of gray at her temples shone in dark blond hair that was pulled up into her standard chignon, and her gray-green eyes swept the room with a glance. She wore a pale blue business suit and black heels.

She and Beth's father had been incredibly close, to the point where sometimes it seemed as if they forgot they'd had five children together. But because of how they'd been raised—including Piper—the Wingate siblings had stuck together, and that closeness remained today.

Ava took a seat at the head of the table and folded her hands together in front of her. "I won't waste time on pleasantries…"

Beth threw a glance at Sutton, who shrugged in answer. Ava *never* wasted time on pleasantries—like *How are you? I've missed you.* Or even *I love you.*

"You all know I've been spending time at the company these last six months," their mom was saying in her clipped tones. "I wanted to get to know each department in turn, get a handle on how things were running."

"Mother," Sebastian interrupted quietly. "Why don't you just tell us what it was that required this meeting?"

"Fine." She looked at all of them, her cool eyes appraising. "I've found a discrepancy in accounting."

"What?" Sutton sat forward, all pretense of casual disinterest gone.

Sebastian, in charge of his siblings and cousins, as always, held up one hand to quiet everyone. His gaze fixed on his mother, he said, "What exactly did you find, Mother?"

"In the simplest terms," Ava told him. "I've discovered money missing. Being quietly, carefully, skimmed from several different accounts."

"How much?" Zeke's question broke the stunned silence.

Ava looked at him directly. "At this point, it's difficult to be sure. But, at a minimum, several hundred thousand dollars."

"What?" Sebastian slapped one hand on the table and Piper jumped. "Sorry," he muttered.

"How long has this been going on?" Beth watched her mother's face and noticed the tightening at the corners of Ava's mouth.

"From what I can tell at this early stage," Ava said, "it's been going on several years."

"Who the hell would do that?" Sutton demanded of no one in particular.

"And how?" Luke asked.

"It couldn't have been easy," Piper murmured.

"Easier than it should have been," Ava said with a quick look at her sister. "Every department is compartmentalized. Every section has their own bookkeeping division. No one knows what's happening anywhere else."

"That was done deliberately," Sebastian reminded her. "Breaking it up seemed the best way to keep everything from being centralized."

"I know. But that plan obviously has its flaws." Ava looked at her oldest son, then included everyone else when she said, "I've decided to hire an outside auditor to go over the books. Once we know how long it's been happening and how much has been stolen, we can look for the thief."

"I'm on board with an auditor," Sebastian murmured, "but we need to keep this quiet. Wingate Enterprises is big business. WinJet alone is a billion-dollar firm. We don't want outsiders worried about the health of Wingate. Until we get to the bottom of this," he added, looking at his siblings and cousins, "we keep this in the family."

"Agreed," Ava said, then looked around the table.

Everyone else concurred and apparently that was enough for Ava. She stood up and added, "Once we know more, we'll meet about this again."

She walked out of the room, and the rest of them were left sitting at the table, staring at each other. Beth looked at Piper. "Did you know about this? Did Mom talk to you first?"

Piper held up both hands and shook her head. "Not a word."

"Auditors," Sutton muttered. "If this is as big as Mom thinks it is, we could be in serious trouble."

"Let's wait for the reports before we panic," Piper told him.

"No one is panicking," Sebastian put in, dropping into his chair again. "But we damn well should start some planning."

Four

Later that day, Cam followed Olivia Turner around the yard and watched her making notes, taking measurements and so many pictures that he wondered why she didn't just take a video and leave it at that.

But he appreciated her thoroughness, too. Olivia's construction company had a great reputation for coming in on time, on budget or under, and her work was always top grade. So whatever estimate she gave him, he'd accept it. Of course, she didn't know that.

"Okay," she said, and turned to face him. She tapped her tablet a few more times, then lifted her gaze to his. "I've got a good idea of what you're going for here, and it's a good plan."

"Thanks. How long to get your estimate on the job?"

She tipped her head to one side, and her bright red braid swung out and across her shoulder. "For the whole job? I mean, for the remodel on the house as well as the guest cottages and everything else?"

"Yeah. All of it."

Her eyebrows shot up and her green eyes narrowed thoughtfully. "That's a big job. You'd basically be hiring my crew for the next six months or more."

He nodded. "I would be. Can you handle that?"

She took a breath, sighed and looked around the land. He knew what she was seeing. Live oaks, open space filled only with the potential of what it could be, and his house, about two hundred yards from where they were standing. He knew she was seeing it as it would be when the job was completed. He liked that. In his experience, a contractor needed to have imagination and vision as well as talent. Hell, he could see it, too, and wanted it done sooner rather than later. Finally she turned to look at him.

"I'd have to hire on more help—and there are two or three jobs I've already lined up," she warned. "I can't leave those people hanging."

"I respect that. The question is," he continued, "can you juggle those jobs and mine, and still give a hundred percent to all of us?"

At that, she straightened up, lifted her chin and

assured him, "I always give a hundred percent. If we take on a job, it gets our best."

"Good to know." He nodded, taking the sting out of his question. He had already known about her reputation, but it was good to have it confirmed. "So. The estimate?"

She laughed. "In a hurry?"

"Yeah," he said, and looked down the path toward the barn and the stables and the fields beyond. He wanted to get going on the next chapter in his life and wasn't one to just stand around waiting. "I am. Can you handle that?"

She laughed. "I grew up with brothers. I can handle pretty much everything." Glancing at her tablet again, she added, "I'll go over these figures and get back to you by day after tomorrow with a firm number."

"A number," he reminded her, "that also includes another stable capable of stalling twelve horses."

She laughed again, shaking her head. "If I stay here much longer, are you going to keep throwing more jobs at me?"

"You never know." Cam turned to glance at his house. "You can leave the remodel of the house to the end. I'd rather have the rest up and running as soon as possible."

"Okay, that works." She paused, then said, "Seems to me, you're rushing to get back into the swing of being in Royal."

"Yeah, you could say that." He'd missed this place while he was in California. And the sooner he was in business and a member of the TCC, the sooner it would feel like he'd never really left.

"Well, if you want to see half of Royal, you should come to the Fire Department Open House this Saturday."

"Is that right?"

Olivia shrugged. "They're raffling off a new truck to raise money to fix up the station and maybe get some new equipment. But there'll be a band and free food and, like I said, no place better for you to mingle with all the people you want to see."

"It's a good idea," he agreed. And it sounded like something Beth would be attending. He wanted to cross paths with her again, and doing it while surrounded by half the town seemed like the safest way to go.

"Great. I'll see you there. You can probably meet most of my crew, too." Then she turned to look at his stable. "Are you wanting basically a copy of the building you already have?"

He grinned. "Basically, but on the interior, I've got a few ideas."

Olivia tossed her braid back over her shoulder, took a breath and said, "Of course you do. Okay, let's hear 'em."

The following day, Beth stood at her office window, staring out at Royal. Her mind was whirling with the implications of her mother's discovery. In fact, the whole family was in an uproar. Who could be stealing from them? She didn't believe for a minute it was anyone in the family. But that meant one of their employees was a thief, and that was hard to fathom, as well.

Her brothers, cousins and mother had been talking about nothing but this situation, and while Beth couldn't blame them, she'd happily come into work and put the worry aside for a while.

Leaving the house today had felt like she was escaping a pressure cooker. Taking care of business on her charities was practically a vacation when compared to the nonstop speculation happening at the ranch.

Since her office was at the end of Main Street, directly opposite City Hall, her view included the landscaped grounds around the 150-year-old building. Summer flowers dazzled in brilliant colors at the bases of the oaks sprinkled across the lawn. There were benches in the shade, allowing places to sit and relax, and at the moment several people were taking advantage of them.

Beth's mind jumped from one subject to the next, as if it couldn't find one specific thought to settle on. It was hard to admit that thinking about a thief at the family company was soothing compared to thinking about Camden Guthrie.

Ridiculous to still be focusing on that *kiss*. But

here she was. Her dreams last night had starred Cam, that bone-melting kiss and then so much more that she'd finally awakened, her body aching with need. Being awake didn't stop the mental torture that her mind gleefully inflicted, though.

Funny that she could remember the fire, the all-consuming heat between them and, at the same time, cruise over the pain she'd experienced when he left town with another woman. That pain had remained for a long time and had colored every relationship since. How could she open her heart to anyone when the one man she'd trusted with *everything* had betrayed her?

"And if I don't stop thinking about Cam, I'm never going to finish working on the Fire Department Open House." Saying it didn't make her leave the window and go back to her desk. Instead, she watched people streaming down the sidewalks.

Then she spotted *him.* Camden Guthrie. As if her hunger had conjured him. Her stomach did a spin and dip, and a curl of heat settled low in her belly. He was wearing jeans, a white button-down shirt, black boots and a gray Stetson. What was it about a man in jeans? And what was it about this one man that could turn her inside out so easily?

Her gaze was fixed on him to the exclusion of everything else in Royal, so when he stopped and looked across the street to her office, she swore their eyes locked. Silly though. He couldn't see her with the glare of the sun, and still she felt a rush of desire that only bristled and grew when he crossed the street, headed her way.

Why did she care? She shouldn't. She'd promised herself she wouldn't. Yet here she was—mouth watering, nerves rattling and her heartbeat thudding heavily in her chest. Desire mingled with regret and the last vestiges of a romance she'd once lost herself in.

He crossed the street in long strides, pushed her door open, stepped inside and swept his hat off. "Beth."

Well, their agreement to stay clear of each other hadn't even lasted twenty-four hours. But then she'd known at the time it was a futile bargain. Like metal shavings to a magnet, Beth had always been drawn to Cam and it looked as though the years that had separated them hadn't done a thing to lessen that draw.

She looked into his dark brown eyes and felt the heat of his body reach across the few feet of space between them. How had she gone fifteen years without seeing him? How would she stay away from him now?

Trying to salvage the situation, not to mention her pride, she said, "Didn't we agree to not be around each other?"

"We did."

"And yet?"

He grinned and her heart tumbled. This was so

much harder than it should have been. Couldn't she just remind herself that he'd married someone else? Someone that Beth had once called a friend? That he'd betrayed her, left Texas for California and had never looked back? Why was her body so eager to forgive him while her mind held on to the painful memories?

"I was at City Hall checking out some building regulations—"

"Okay," she said, interrupting him. "But why are you *here*?"

He reached into his shirt pocket, pulled out a cashier's check and handed it to her. "I stopped at the bank earlier so I could make good on my part of our deal."

Right. Their other deal. Not about staying apart, but about getting him into the TCC. Fine. That was good. She was pleased. Really. He wasn't here to kiss her again—he was simply here to wrap up a business deal. She unfolded the check, glanced at the amount and gasped.

Astonished, she looked up at him. "A hundred thousand dollars?"

One eyebrow arched. "Not enough?"

"No. I mean yes." She shook her head, took a breath, and when she could speak again without babbling, she said, "It is enough. It's more than generous. I wasn't expecting so much."

And didn't know what to make of it. Was he doing

this just to help? Or was he trying to impress her? Because he had.

He grinned briefly and reached for the check. "I'm happy to take it back and give you less."

Beth whipped the check into the pocket of her cream-colored capris and shook her head. She might be confused about a lot of things at the moment, but on this, she was perfectly clear. "Oh, no, you don't. This is great. It's going to make a huge difference for the children's wing. Seriously, thanks."

"Not a problem."

She kept her gaze locked on his and tried to read what she saw there. But he was stoic, hiding whatever was running through his mind. Was the donation his only reason for stopping in? And why did she hope it wasn't? Had she learned *nothing* in the last fifteen years? He'd left and she'd stayed, building a life. And she was damn good at it.

It had taken a lot of work, but she had thrived without Cam. Was she really willing to put all of that aside in favor of the kind of passion she remembered so vividly?

Yes, she knew he was no longer the simple ranch hand she'd once loved. Knew he had money. But, really, she'd never thought about how rich he actually was now. What else had changed? She wondered what her father would make of the man he was so sure would amount to nothing more than a "ranch hand."

“So now you’ll talk to the TCC membership board?”

She came up out of her thoughts and told herself to pay attention. “I will. That was our deal.” She’d stop by today to see Burt Wheeler, Cam’s father-in-law. Just thinking that gave her a twinge of…what? Regret? Envy? Cam had married Julie Wheeler and lived a life with her that Beth had once thought would be hers. It felt small and petty to be jealous of a dead woman, but that didn’t change what she was feeling.

At the same time, though, she had to wonder if Beth and Cam had run off together so long ago, would things have worked out the way they had? Would he be a successful entrepreneur? Would she be working for the family corporation? She’d never know. More questions with no answers.

“While I’m here, there’s something else I wanted to talk to you about,” he said, and she noticed him turning the brim of his hat in his hands.

Was this what the big check had been about? To soften her up for whatever else was coming? He looked nervous. But that couldn’t be the case. After all, Cam had never had trouble going after exactly what he wanted. It’s one of the things she’d found so exciting about him.

“What is it?”

“You don’t have to sound so suspicious.” He smiled and shook his head. “Are you so much like your father now that you’re wary of everything?”

Another stab at her late father, but on this one she could agree. Her dad had looked at everything with a cynical eye. Including—maybe *especially*—Camden Guthrie. She had been the daughter of a very wealthy man, and Cam was the son of horse trainers. Trent had never trusted Cam, and once he left town, Beth had asked herself if she shouldn't have been more like her father. Still, she couldn't blame Cam for holding on to a grudge against the man who'd thought of him as not worthy.

But if Cam didn't understand that her cynicism where he was concerned had more to do with what *he* had done to her than anything her father had done, then he was being deliberately oblivious.

"No," she said at last. "It's not my dad who affected my trust issues. I learned fifteen years ago to be wary of people."

His eyes flashed, and she knew she'd scored a hit. Somehow, it didn't give her the sense of satisfaction she'd been expecting. What good would it do her to throw proverbial stones? Holding up one hand for peace, she said, "Sorry. Never mind all that. Just tell me what you wanted to talk to me about."

Nodding slowly, he kept his dark eyes on hers. Beth could have warmed herself with the heat in them. "All right. It's about the other deal we made yesterday."

"You mean keeping our distance from each

other?" She laughed shortly. "Yeah, since you're here, that one clearly isn't working so far."

"And it won't, either." He held on to his hat with one hand and tapped it idly against his left thigh. "Avoiding each other isn't going to work. I'm home to stay, Beth, so we're going to be seeing each other plenty. What're we supposed to do, run and hide every time we spot each other on Main Street? Because I'm not doing that."

Running and hiding were the furthest things from her mind right now, too. "Me, either. Okay, what's your solution?"

"That we do the opposite," he said bluntly. "Instead of avoiding each other, we start spending time together."

Her stomach spun. She was having a hard enough time around Cam as it was. Spending more time with him would only make that more difficult—not easier. "And that solves…what?"

"It gets us used to each other again," he said. "Accustomed to being together and *not* giving in to the attraction between us. With any luck, after some time passes, that'll cool off."

Not from where she was standing. Just having him in her office was lighting up her insides and making her blood burn and bubble. The way he was standing so stiffly, so obviously filled with tension, told her that he was feeling the burn, too. "You think so?"

"I do. We keep our hands off each other, but hang out, and we'll get past this…need."

"Seems risky."

"I can do it if you can."

A challenge. He'd always known the way to get to her. Tell Beth she *couldn't* do something and she would find a way to accomplish it. "Why couldn't I? You're not completely irresistible, Camden."

That was a lie because, yes, he was. At least he always had been to Beth. But she wouldn't be admitting to that anytime soon. She still wanted him, and she probably always would. However, she'd learned the hard way a long time ago that want and need didn't translate into forever. And she wasn't about to set herself up for more pain.

"If that's how you really feel," he said, "then this shouldn't be a problem for either of us."

Well, he'd boxed her in neatly there. If she said no, he'd realize that she didn't trust herself around him. If she said yes, then she was taking a chance she might be sorry for. Yet, what choice did either of them have? They were going to be seeing each other around town for the rest of their lives. If he actually stayed in Royal. Wasn't it a better idea to learn how to do that without opening up old wounds?

She took a deep breath to steady herself. It didn't work. "Okay then, we'll try it your way."

"Good. Now, on that, I've got a plan."

"Of course you do."

His mouth curved in a slow smile and flames licked at her core. Oh, this was *so* not a good idea.

"The word around Royal is that you had a big hand in setting up your family's offices. You know, not decorating exactly, but—"

At least they were on safe ground here. "You mean designing the interiors for function and style?"

He snorted. "Okay, I wouldn't have used those words, but yeah. Well, I'd like you to help me out with my project at the ranch."

Intrigued in spite of everything, Beth felt a tug of interest, but she had to tell him, "I'm not a licensed interior designer, you know."

"I don't care about that." He glanced around her office and then back to her. "You've got a good eye, and that would help me out a lot."

She knew what he saw when he looked at the space she'd created. Beth was proud of her work here and at her brothers' offices. In her own place, she'd simply taken the space available and made it more her own with the bookcases, tables, chairs and plants that spilled out of brass pots. She didn't own the building, so she wasn't able to do all she would have, given the chance. Still, the atmosphere was rich but homey, and put people at ease the moment they walked in.

In her brothers' offices, though, she'd been able to affect how they were remodeled. Hidden bathrooms, large work area, with window placement to expand the view and the feel of openness. Then the flooring, the paint and the accessories that made an office more personal, less industrial chic.

Beth had to ask, "What exactly did you have in mind?"

"I told you about the dude ranch project I'm going to be setting up."

"Yes…"

He walked farther into the room and looked around. Beth's gaze followed him and she saw his eyes slide over her desk, the framed family photos, then he turned his gaze back to hers. "I've hired Olivia Turner to build a dozen guest cottages to start."

"To *start*?"

He gave her an all too brief grin that lit up his eyes. "Yeah. Thought I'd start out small. See how it goes. I can always add more in a year or two if I want to."

Beth knew the Circle K well, so she was aware that there was more than enough room for what he was planning. And Olivia Turner would do a great job. "How do I fit into all this?"

He leaned one shoulder against the wall, hooked one foot over the other ankle and said, "I was thinking you could work with me. Make those cabins… special. Something out of the ordinary. I want them to stand out from any other outfit like it. Hell, from every other dude ranch in the West. Olivia will build them, but I want her to have some specific ideas to work with."

She stared up into his eyes and told herself that this would be a mistake. Working closely with him was just too much temptation. But a small voice in her mind whispered if she was going to prove to herself *and* to Cam that she was well and truly over him, wasn't this the best way to do it? To be tempted and not surrender? Couldn't she use this as a lesson for herself? And, yes, she knew she was mentally trying to find a way to do this because it sounded like fun.

"Working together could be dangerous, Cam."

"No. It's just the first test in our new bargain." He pushed away from the wall to stand up straight right in front of her. He looked down at her and said, "Really? You think we can't control ourselves? Are we still eighteen and full of hormones?"

"No." *Yes.*

"We're both adults," he continued. "I think we can restrain ourselves. Are you worried?"

That was a direct challenge and she knew it. "Not about me..." He was so close she could have laid her palm on his chest and felt his heart pounding. She could have gone up on her toes and laid her mouth over his. She did neither.

He nodded. "Fine. An amendment to the new bargain. I won't make a move until you do."

It was her turn to laugh, though it sounded a little strained, even to Beth. "That's not going to happen."

"Then there's nothing to worry about, is there?"

Oh, there was so much here to worry about. "I guess not."

"So you'll do it."

"Yes."

One corner of his mouth tipped up. "Great. Come out to the ranch tomorrow and I'll show you what I'm thinking."

"I can't be there until afternoon," she said, mentally flipping through her appointments and obligations.

"That'll work. I've got that Longhorn herd arriving early in the day. I'll be able to get away by afternoon."

In spite of her bravado, Beth knew that being around Cam was going to be torture. The memories of his touch, his kiss, were too fresh now. Before he'd returned, those images from fifteen years ago had been watery, misty pictures in her mind. Like a Monet, beautiful but indistinct.

Now everything was crystal clear again. She knew how he felt pressed up against her. The taste of him clung to her lips, and she could nearly feel his strong hands sweeping up and down her spine. Heat coiled inside her, a spring ever tightening, ready to snap. And it wouldn't take much to push her past the point of no return. So, was this foolish? No doubt. Was she going to do it anyway? Absolutely.

When the door opened behind Cam, Beth jolted,

tore her gaze from his and nearly let her internal groan slip out.

Justin McCoy stood there, his gaze fixed on Cam. In a split second, she compared the two men and Justin definitely came up short. He was tall but soft, his belly already a little paunchy. His skin was pale, his eyes a watery blue and he kept his white-blond hair cut short to obscure the fact that he was already losing it. He was a wealthy rancher who never went out on his own land. He had "people" for that.

Looking at the two men now, Beth couldn't imagine why she'd ever gone out with Justin in the first place. She guessed she'd been lonely enough to take a chance. And she'd known almost from the first that it wasn't going to be what Justin was hoping for. Once they'd had sex, she was sure of it. There'd been no fire. No flash of desire so overwhelming you couldn't breathe. No desperation to touch and be touched. Just a mildly interesting half hour that was quickly forgotten.

She'd dated Justin on and off for a while, but called an end to it a few months ago because he wanted a commitment from her that Beth couldn't give. She didn't love him and wouldn't even consider marrying him. Still, Justin wasn't one to take no for an answer.

"Justin. Hi, this is a surprise." Not an altogether happy one, either.

"I was over at City Hall," he said, walking to her

side. “Thought I’d stop in and see if I could take you to lunch.”

Beth realized that, although he was talking to her, he was looking at Cam. The two men were practically bristling as they gave each other challenging stares. Best to end this now.

“Oh, I’m sorry. I’m too busy to take lunch today,” she said.

“Is that right?” He was still staring at Cam.

She sighed. “Justin, you remember Camden Guthrie, don’t you? He’s just moved back home recently.”

“Oh,” he said quietly, “I remember him.”

“I was going to say the same thing.” Cam’s features were grim, his voice a low rumble.

“Aren’t you the one who ran off with Burt Wheeler’s daughter, Julie?”

Cam’s jaw tightened and Beth breathed deeply. She had always been able to tell when Cam’s temper was beginning to spike. His eyes were narrowed and flashing out a danger sign.

“I am,” he said. “Aren’t you the one who was kicked off the football team for cheating on your biology exam?”

“I didn’t cheat.”

Cam glared at the other man. “You did. In more ways than one.”

Justin’s pale cheeks flushed with barely contained rage, and Beth wondered what Cam was talking about. Now wasn’t the time to find out, though.

"Okay." She spoke into the tense silence that followed. "I think that's enough testosterone poisoning for today. Cam, maybe you should go."

Both eyebrows rose when he looked at her. "You want me to leave?"

"Please."

Justin looked smug that she'd chosen to have him stay, but that wasn't the reason she'd asked Cam to go instead of him. It was simply that she'd known Cam would do as she asked and had been positive that Justin wouldn't have.

Cam nodded, with one last, hard look at Justin. "All right. I'll go." He shifted a glance to Beth. "I'll see you tomorrow?"

"Yes," she said, though she knew that wouldn't make Justin happy. Not her problem.

Once Cam was gone, Beth looked up at Justin and saw his eyes flash with irritation,

"Justin, thanks for the lunch offer, but I really am too busy today."

He ignored that and groused, "I don't think it's appropriate for a nearly engaged woman to be alone with Guthrie's kind of man."

That she hadn't expected. Even leaving aside the *nearly engaged woman* thing for a moment. "Excuse me?" Beth blinked at him. "Guthrie's 'kind of man'?"

"Money doesn't buy class. He's still the same as he was in school."

"All of us are, apparently," she muttered. She clearly remembered Justin and his friends trying to bully Cam because he was half Native American, but they hadn't succeeded because Cam had never cared what anyone had had to say about him. He just went on with his life and fought back only when he was forced into it.

"Justin, I'll be alone with anyone I choose. You're not in charge of who I speak to. And, more importantly—" she paused for emphasis "—I really want you to hear me on this… We are *not* engaged."

"As good as," he argued.

"Not even close," Beth said firmly. Honestly, she hadn't wanted to hurt Justin's feelings, so she'd dated him for far too long. She hadn't wanted to be mean when she turned down his proposal, and he'd interpreted that as uncertainty. Now she was done. "We're never going to be engaged, Justin. In spite of the fact that you simply won't listen to me."

"Beth, I've been more than tolerant of your indecision, but I believe I'm running out of patience."

Talking to Justin was exhausting. Like beating your head against a steel wall trying to make a hole. All that happened was a headache.

"As am I," she said, suddenly so tired of this whole thing that all she could think of was to get rid of Justin so she could have some peace. If the man wouldn't respond to her polite refusals, maybe it was time to be less polite. "And I haven't been indecisive.

I've told you repeatedly that I wasn't interested in a relationship and nothing has changed. We're not engaged. We're not going to be. No one tells me who I can speak to. And I don't want to go to lunch."

He gave her a sadly indulgent look. "Beth, honey, ladies don't show their tempers."

"Oh, for heaven's sake, Justin!"

He frowned, more disappointed. He tucked both thumbs behind his oversize silver belt buckle and said gently, "Now Beth, honey, calm down."

"Telling someone to calm down does not calm them down, just so you know."

He only stared at her. "What was Guthrie doing here?"

Beth sighed and said, "Cam's an old…friend."

"Yeah, I know all about that. I live here, remember?"

"Okay, Justin, the truth is Cam dropped off a donation to the children's wing at the hospital."

His mouth worked and she could see the muscle in his jaw twitch as he ground his teeth. "Fine. But I don't think it's appropriate for you to be alone with your ex, Beth. People know we're a couple and—"

"Justin, we're *not* a couple." She shook her head as she bit back on her annoyance. "I've explained this to you already. Multiple times. Including just two minutes ago. We are not together and we're not going to be."

Sunlight sliding through the front window slanted

across that hideous belt buckle and nearly blinded her. She took a step back just to keep her vision clear.

"I'm sorry, Justin, but I think you should go now."

She didn't even watch him leave.

Five

"You sure you want me to wait in the car?"

Beth sighed, glanced at Gracie and looked back at Burt Wheeler's ranch house. Truthfully, she'd rather have Gracie's company. Heck, she'd rather not be here at all. But a deal was a deal, And since she'd be seeing Cam later today, she was here to hold up her end of their bargain.

"Yeah, if you're out here, I can use you as my excuse to leave quickly if I have to." Beth smiled at her. "Keep the AC running if you want, but parking under this old oak should help with the heat."

"I'll be fine," Gracie said, reaching into her bag for her tablet. "I'll go over the donations list while I wait."

"God, you're good." Another sigh. She really wished she could trade places with Gracie, But she climbed out of the car and walked across the yard to the Wheelers' white Victorian ranch house.

It was in beautiful shape, with a freshly painted, swept porch with bright blue tables and chairs sprinkled along its length. The window glass shone in the sun, and there was a summer wreath hanging on the front door. She knocked and waited and, when Burt opened the door, steeled herself for the conversation to come.

"Beth Wingate," he said, his voice a gravel road. "What're you doing out here?"

"I've got a favor to ask, Burt," she answered brightly. "Can I come in?"

"Sure." He stepped back, a big man with a rounded belly, a full gray beard and a gleaming bald head. His brown eyes were curious as he steered her into the living room.

Burt's wife's stamp was all over the house. Overstuffed pastel furniture was gathered in conversational knots. Polished tables, family photos on the walls—Beth's gaze went directly to a shot of Julie Wheeler with her brothers. Her fun-filled smile was frozen in time, and it must tear at the Wheelers whenever they looked at it. She shifted her gaze back to Julie's father when he started talking.

"My Dottie's in town at the market..."

"I didn't come to see your wife, Burt," Beth said,

though she had to admit this conversation would have been easier if Dottie Wheeler had been there. "It's you I need to talk to."

"Sounds serious." He crossed his arms over his broad chest, tucked his chin in and watched her warily. "What's this about?"

"It's about Cam Guthrie," she blurted.

His features turned instantly to stone. "I've got nothing to say about him."

"I understand, Burt, but—" She'd known it would be hard, but Beth could see both anger and pain in the older man's eyes, and she regretted causing it.

"You don't understand," he interrupted. "You can't. Only me, Dottie and Julie's brothers do. That man ran off with my baby girl. Took her away from her family. From her home. And then let her die out in that godless city in California."

Julie had died of cancer. It must have been horrible for her family—and for Cam. But it was hardly Cam's fault. "Burt…"

"No." He shook his head, and if he'd had hair, it would have whipped around like a lion's mane. "Whatever he wants from me, he doesn't get."

His voice, already rough and deep, got louder, and flags of red appeared on his cheeks. Beth wasn't afraid of him, but she was a little worried that he might have a heart attack. Burt was well-known for his temper and for his ability to cut people down to size with a sharp tongue that took no prisoners. But she wasn't going to be intimidated, no matter how much she might be sympathizing with him.

"Whether we like it or not, Cam's back in Royal now," she said in spite of his anger. "He wants to join the TCC and you're the membership chair."

"I am and I'll vote no on letting him in," he assured her. "He got my little girl pregnant! High school kids is all they were and she was pregnant!"

Beth swayed under that blow. Julie was *pregnant*? How had she never heard a whisper of that rumor? And how could Cam insist he hadn't cheated on Beth, if he had married Julie because she was pregnant? And if she had been pregnant, where was the child? How many lies were flying around Royal these days? Oh, she really was almost as furious as Burt, yet the hurt she felt dwarfed the rage.

"Didn't know about that, did you?" His voice dropped as if he was sympathizing with her now. "Well, we didn't spread it around. Only her mother and me and Camden Guthrie knew the truth. We didn't even tell her brothers."

Beth swallowed past the knot of humiliation lodged in her throat and wondered how many more times Cam was going to slice at her heart. Why hadn't he at least told her the truth before asking her to speak to his father-in-law? Why hadn't he given her all the information she needed so she wouldn't be caught like this? She breathed deeply and said the only thing she could. "It was fifteen years ago, Burt."

"You think our pain *ends*?"

"Of course not." Hers hadn't. Why would Burt and Dottie's? "But Julie and Cam made their decision a long time ago."

"So it was my girl's fault?" His eyes were wide with astonishment.

"I didn't say that. But Cam didn't force her to run. She went with him, as hard as that is to accept. She was with Cam. She ran away with him and stayed with him willingly." Beth wanted to blame Cam alone and so did Burt. But the truth was Julie had been a part of it all from the beginning. It took *two* to make a baby. And that thought twisted her heart until it was nothing more than a painful lump in her chest. He'd made a baby with Julie while making plans with Beth. How had she missed it?

Now is not the time, she told herself. "Burt, all Cam wants is a fair shot at joining the TCC."

"He'll have that," Burt said hotly, and ran his palm across the top of his head. "He has the right to apply for membership. Like I said, he won't have my vote, but it's not my place to block him from the club."

Cam would have to accept that, Beth told herself, because it was the best he was going to get from Burt Wheeler. Burt was well-known about town as a bully…loud and aggressive, but he was also a father still in pain at the tragic loss of his daughter. Beth reached out and laid one hand on his forearm.

"Thank you, Burt."

He jerked a nod.

"And I'm really sorry about everything. About dredging this up."

"You're a nice girl, Beth." He blew out a pent-up breath and gave her hand an awkward pat. Gruffly he said, "Your daddy was a pain in the ass, but you're a nice girl. And you didn't dredge up anything. Julie is always with me."

She couldn't blame him for not liking her father. Many people hadn't, including his own kids most of the time. As for the rest, she understood what he meant in saying that Julie was always with him. Cam had always been with her, too. Did that make her a fool?

As she left the Wheeler house, she was already planning just what she would have to say to Camden Guthrie.

Camden worked through the morning, hoping to ease his mind by concentrating on a single task—making sure the Longhorn cattle arrived safely to take their place on the Circle K rangeland. A couple of days ago, his ranch hands had temporarily fenced in a two-acre plot where the Longhorns could rest up for a day or two. Cam wanted to make sure they were all healthy and strong enough to be turned out to graze.

In spite of his mind twisting with thoughts of Beth—and the shock of seeing her with Justin

McCoy of all damn people—he smiled as he watched the most quintessential Texas breed of cattle stepping down the ramps of the cattle truck. The Longhorns were wildly diverse in color: no two were alike, and the spread of their horns ranged from four feet to nearly nine.

The rattle of their hooves on metal and the clack of their horns slapping together filled the air. He caught more than a couple of the cowboys grinning like children just watching the legendary cattle slowly claim their new home.

"They're really something, aren't they, boss?" Henry Jordan sat his horse right beside Cam, and both men stared out at the cattle.

"They really are." It was a damn miracle the breed had been saved back in the 1920s. People had been smart enough to realize that crossbreeding with imported cattle was going to destroy the one breed that had evolved on their own to survive and thrive on the range without any help from humans.

"My boys are loving this. They've never seen a Longhorn up close," Henry said, pointing to where his three teenage sons were working the herd with the other cowboys.

"A lot of people haven't, Henry," Cam replied, leaning both hands on the pommel of his saddle. "But we're going to fix that with the dude ranch. Our tourists are going to get a glimpse of the real Texas."

His starting herd was small—two hundred head,

with a lot of females and yearlings. It wouldn't take long for the herd to expand, and Cam welcomed it. He had plenty of open land for them to graze. All the ranch hands had to do was make sure they didn't drift onto the land reserved for the Black Angus cattle. Damned if he'd allow crossbreeding on his own ranch.

"The vet suggested we leave the herd penned in for at least a couple of days. Quarantine to make sure they're all healthy and give them time to eat and get their strength back after the travel." Even a two-day trip was hard on cattle. "You guys keep an eye on the herd, and by early next week, we'll move them down to the south pasture."

"You got it." Henry tipped the brim of his hat, then rode off to join the others.

Cam watched it all for a few more minutes, then headed back to the house to get his truck. He had one more appointment before meeting Beth that afternoon.

Seeing her at her office had cost him nearly every damn ounce of his self-control. It had taken all he had to keep from reaching for her. And what the hell was she doing with Justin McCoy hanging around? Scowling to himself, he kicked his horse into a gallop, hoping to drive that image out of his head.

McCoy was a snake and Cam had more reason than most to know it. Was Beth really foolish enough to hook herself up with that bastard? Because if she was, he'd be happy to step in and tell her the cold, hard truth about Justin McCoy.

Beth. It all came down to Beth. She was the same and yet so different. She wasn't the open, laughing girl he'd once known. She'd grown, as he had. They'd changed and maybe that was best. It forced them both to get to know the people they were now—not just to depend on what had once been.

Beth had built herself a good life here and he admired that. He'd done well, too, so in that regard, they were on equal footing. Not like back in the day when she'd been a Wingate princess and he was a working cowboy.

Today she was so much more. Hell, he hadn't been able to think about anything but her for days. Her smile. Her scent. The taste of her. The way her eyes snapped with indignation when her temper was up. He'd missed her. In spite of his marriage to Julie, he'd never forgotten Beth.

The guilt of that had nibbled on him for years. And now thinking about Beth the way he was had that same guilt growing and snapping at him with razor-sharp teeth.

He'd known coming home to Royal wouldn't be a walk in the park, but damned if he'd figured that Beth would once again tangle him up in knots.

Naturally, the Royal Diner was crowded, and that was fine with Cam. He noticed people watching him, heard the whispers as he passed, and he paid them all no attention. Cam could put up with the staring and whispering. For a while.

Tony Alvarez was sitting at a booth overlooking Main Street, and Cam slid onto the bench seat opposite him. Tony's black hair was cut short, his brown eyes were sharp and his quick grin was the best welcome home Cam had had so far.

Sticking his right hand out, Tony said, "Damn, it's good to see you."

"You, too." Cam shook hands with his old friend, then eased back into the booth. "Been too long."

"Well, that's what happens when you move to California and get rich and famous."

"Look who's talking," Cam said, laughing. His old friend had played Major League Baseball and had made a hell of a name for himself before retiring.

Tony waved that off. "I played a game and got paid for it. You got on TV for knowing how to build things."

"I wasn't really famous," he said. His and Julie's show had done well for two years, but it was one of a dozen remodel shows. Then Julie had gotten sick, and everything ended.

"Rich though." Tony grinned again.

Cam laughed because Tony had always been the guy who said exactly what he was thinking. Even back in high school, you always knew just where you stood with him. It was a trait Cam admired and he was glad his old friend hadn't changed.

And, yes, he'd gotten richer than he'd ever thought possible. When he was a kid, he'd figured that making his own fortune would solve all of his problems. Yet now that he had more money than he could spend in two lifetimes, he knew money didn't solve anything. Made things easier, for damn sure, but the problems you had, you would still have. You'd just drive a better car and live in a bigger house.

Amanda Battles stepped up to the booth just then. "Hi, Tony." Her gaze shifted. "Cam. It's good to see you home."

"Thanks." He smiled and meant it. "I appreciate it."

"Nate tells me you're doing a lot of work on the old Circle K."

"I am," Cam said, sliding a glance at his friend.

"Good." She nodded. "That tells me you're here to stay." Pulling an old-fashioned order pad out of her pocket, she poised her pen over it and asked, "What can we get you two?"

Once they'd both ordered, Amanda left them alone and Tony asked, "So what did you want to talk about?"

Cam sat back and laid his right arm along the top of the red vinyl booth bench. In high school, Tony and Cam had been best friends. They'd played on the championship baseball team and both had dreamed of making the bigs. The only difference between them was that Tony had actually made it. He'd played eight seasons for Houston before blowing out a knee, which had ended his career.

But Tony being Tony, that hadn't stopped him from finding success somewhere else.

"Are you still running that baseball camp of yours?"

"Oh, hell yes," Tony said with a smile. "Thanks, Pam," he murmured when Amanda's sister brought them both cups of coffee. Then back to Cam, he said, "It's bigger than ever. We've got forty kids lined up for this coming winter. Twenty in the first camp and twenty more in the second. I'm still renting the land we operate on. Soon though, I'm going to have to look for more land. Build a permanent site. Maybe hold camps all winter and up to spring training."

He held the coffee mug cupped in his palms. "I'm thinking about doing a dream team thing for adults, too. Get the older guys who used to fantasize about playing big-league ball out to meet some players and have some fun."

Cam nodded, thinking. Tony's baseball camp had started out small about five years ago. Cam might not have been living in Royal, but that didn't mean he hadn't kept up with what his friends were doing. And in the last five years, Tony's business had really grown. Not only did he have the reputation on his own, but every year his old teammates showed up to impress the kids and to help them work on their games.

"That sounds great," Cam said. "Maybe I'll sign up, too."

Tony looked surprised. "Shoulder good enough?"

He rolled his right shoulder and smiled. "I can't throw the hundred-mile-an-hour fastball anymore, but I can hold my own."

"Good to know. So why are you asking about the camp?"

Cam shrugged, then grinned. "You said you're looking for a more permanent camp?"

"Yeah."

"As it happens, I've got twenty acres at my place that's available."

Tony paused with the coffee cup halfway to his mouth. "Are you serious?"

"Why not?" Cam leaned forward, bracing his elbows on the laminate table. "I'm looking at building a sort of 'dude ranch' at my place."

Tony stared at him for a second or two, then laughed. "No way. Why the hell would you want to do that? Cater to tourists and wannabe cowboys?"

In spite of his friend's words, Camden laughed. "Why not? I'll be running herds on the ranch—had some Longhorns arrive just yesterday…"

"Now that's cool."

"It is," he agreed. "But the thing is, when I was living in California, that place was so crowded, so jammed with people, some days it felt like you couldn't draw a breath.

"And every time someone found out I was from Texas, inevitably, their reaction was, *Oh, I've always dreamed of living on a ranch. Being under the stars.* And every other cliché you can think of."

"Yeah." Tony smiled up at Pam as she delivered his slice of apple pie. "They never think about all the work that goes into ranching."

"Exactly!" Cam glanced at their server and thanked her for his blackberry cobbler. When Pam was gone, he started talking again. "So the idea is to give city people the chance to live like country people, a week at a time. We can do riding lessons. Have bonfires at night, chuck wagon food..."

Tony took a bite of pie, chewed and swallowed. "And how does my baseball camp for kids fit into that?"

"Easy." Cam waved his fork at his buddy as he warmed to his subject. "We could be a big help to each other. Your baseball players might see the ranch and decide to come back. My tourists might like baseball."

Tony snorted a laugh. "Well, who doesn't like baseball?"

"Exactly." Cam grinned again and took a forkful of the cobbler. Meanwhile, he could see Tony thinking this through, and he was pretty sure his old friend was going to go for it.

Wouldn't hurt to sweeten the pie, though. "You know, with twenty acres, you could build a regulation diamond, a couple batting cages, pitching areas… and some bunkhouses for your campers to stay in."

"Hmm. That would be good."

"Think about it," Cam urged. "Where do the campers stay now?"

"At the inn outside of Royal," Tony admitted. "It would make it easier to have them all on-site…"

"Damn right it would." Cam had him and he knew it. Hell, he didn't need Tony's camp to be on the ranchland, but it'd be fun. And that in itself was a good enough reason.

"Hell, you could build yourself a house on the land and provide housing for all of your employees, too."

His friend's eyebrows arched at the suggestion and Cam could practically see the wheels in his mind turning.

Tony cut off another bite of pie and said, "You knew I'd say yes, didn't you?"

Cam shrugged. "You haven't said yes yet."

Laughing, Tony said, "Hell, of course it's yes."

"Great." They shook hands on it, then Cam said, "Why don't you come out to the ranch right now? We can plot out your twenty acres, then call Olivia Turner to tell her she's got another job to do."

Beth and Gracie had their list of potential donors to the silent auction to be held at the TCC masquerade ball in October. They'd already gotten promises from several of the business owners in town, but there were many more to contact.

After her visit with Burt, Beth didn't really feel up to the task of talking to a lot of people. But this was her job and she was going to do it well. She wouldn't let Cam affect the life she'd built. Besides, once this task was finished, she'd be talking to him about all of this and she'd have her answers then.

"Do you want to split the list right down the middle?" Gracie asked. "I'll take the bottom half, you take the top?"

"That would probably be the best way to do it," Beth admitted. Then she looked at Gracie and smiled. "But it's more fun when we go together."

"True." Gracie laughed and reached for her cell phone when it rang. She glanced at the screen, then slid the phone back into her purse.

Beth sent her a questioning look. "You don't have to take it?"

"No, it's just my mom," Gracie said. "She's probably calling to tell me she and my brother have made it to Galveston safely."

Beth sighed. "A week at the beach. Sounds like heaven right now." Especially because it would get her out of Royal and away from Cam so she could do some serious thinking.

"I know. Mom loves the ocean so much I hate that she can't be there more often." Then Gracie gave a sharp nod. "When I win the PowerBall lottery, the first thing I'm going to do is buy Mom a huge house on the beach in Florida. She'd be near her sister, and that would make her happy, too."

Smiling, Beth said, "Big plans."

"Dreams," Gracie corrected wryly. "But dreams are wonderful, aren't they?"

Hers used to be, Beth admitted silently. When she was a girl, she'd dreamed of a life with Cam. Of owning their own ranch and raising kids and horses. Eventually she had woken up and her dreams had dissolved under a good coating of reality. Still, this wasn't about her own shattered illusions.

"You bet. So, when you buy your mom that big house in Florida, are you going to move with her?"

Gracie flipped her long dark hair over her shoulder and shook her head. "No. Royal is home. I'd miss the people. My job. And—" She broke off as if worried she'd said too much. Then she added, "I wouldn't want to leave..."

There was something she wasn't saying and Beth studied her friend for a long moment or two before it dawned on her. "You've got a man and you haven't told me anything about him!"

"What?" Gracie looked at her, wide-eyed, shaking her head. "Who said anything about a man? I'm talking about my job. You. Royal."

"And a man." Beth laughed a little and drew the younger woman to a stop on the sidewalk. "Don't even try to deny it. Your eyes went all gooey for a second."

"I do not get gooey."

"Sadly, we all do at some point," Beth argued. "So spill. Who is this mystery man?"

Gracie sighed and looked around before fixing her gaze on Beth's again. "Nobody. At least, not for me. He doesn't know I'm alive."

Insulted on Gracie's behalf, Beth started talking. "Impossible. You're gorgeous. And smart. And amazing."

"Said my friend, being completely objective."

"Fine." Beth smiled at her. "So if you like this guy so much, why don't you tell him?"

Gracie shook her head firmly. "No, I can't do that."

"Oh, Gracie..."

"Beth, I know you mean well." Gracie winced and looked uncomfortable. "But can we not? I don't want to talk about him. Much less *think* about him."

"Sure. Case closed," Beth said. "Mostly because I know exactly how you feel."

She knew what it was like to be drawn to someone in spite of knowing it was futile. After all, she hadn't been able to smother her feelings for Cam even though she knew she should. So she really wasn't in any position to give relationship advice.

"So for the rest of the day," she said, hooking her

arm through Gracie's, "*men* are off the conversational table."

"But just today, right?" Gracie smiled at her.

"Absolutely," Beth replied. "Come tomorrow, I make no promises."

"Good to know. Hey." Gracie pointed. "There's one of Lauren Roberts's food trucks. Didn't you say you wanted to talk to her about a donation?"

"Yes, I did." Beth looked at the side of the truck and grinned. Gracie Diaz was really good to spend time with. Even though Beth's heart was aching and her mind spinning with way too many thoughts and unanswered questions, she was able to enjoy herself. "Besides, tacos for lunch sounds good, doesn't it?"

Lauren was a fabulous chef and her food trucks were making a real impact on Royal. Luckily, Lauren herself was working the taco truck. When Beth got to the front of the line to order, she grinned up at the woman.

Lauren's shoulder-length dark brown hair was pulled back into a ponytail. She wore a pale blue T-shirt and jeans, and the two women working with her looked pretty much the same.

"Hi, Lauren. Can we get two taco plates and a couple bottles of water?"

She smiled. "Sure. How's it going, Beth? Gracie."

"Fine," Gracie answered. "We're out gathering donations for the TCC masquerade ball in October."

Lauren slid a suspicious glance at Beth as she

made change from the twenty Beth had handed her. "And?"

"And..." Beth went on to say. "I was thinking you might want to donate one of your food trucks for a night. Say someone has a party and you could cater it..."

Lauren worked while she thought about that, and the scents wafting from the truck were making Beth even hungrier. The fact that there were two other women working the stove and the prep area was something else Beth liked about Lauren's business. She hired women to work for her, paid a great wage and gave them experience they could take anywhere.

"It would be great advertising for you," Gracie put in. "Plus it's for a good cause. The children's wing of the hospital."

"Oh, I know..." Lauren looked over Beth's head at the line gathering up behind her. "But to be honest, giving away catering for a party could get out of hand quickly. I don't know if I can afford to donate enough food for a party of sixty or something."

"She's got a good point," Gracie said, and lifted one shoulder in a shrug, as she looked to Beth.

"Okay, what if we put a limit on what people can get?" Beth could see this being a really sought after prize, so she would just have to make Lauren see how brilliant it was. "What if we say you will donate catering for a party of ten? Can you do that?"

Lauren took the two taco plates from the woman

working beside her and handed them down to Beth and Gracie. Then she got the water and passed it over, as well. "Ten?" She thought about it for a second, then nodded. "I can do that. They can even have their choice of food for the party."

"Excellent! Thank you so much, Lauren."

"You're welcome. Enjoy your lunch."

"We will." Beth nodded at Gracie and they moved aside to let the line surge forward. Finding an empty bench on the shady side of the bank building, they sat and toasted each other with icy water, tacos and Spanish rice.

Deliberately Beth kept her thoughts from straying to Camden Guthrie. Her confrontation with him would come soon enough.

Six

At Cam's ranch, he and Tony were checking out the land he was going to lease his old friend. He could have just given him the land or even sold it to him outright. But this way was better—taxwise, for Tony's growing business.

"It's been a long time since I was on a horse," Tony admitted ruefully. "I'll be lucky to walk tomorrow."

Cam laughed. Tugging his Stetson down lower over his eyes, he braced his hands on the pommel of his saddle and stared out at the property. "Horseback is the best way to see the land," he said with satisfaction. Then he shot a quick grin at his pal. "Besides, you're a Texan man, have some pride."

"Oh, I've got plenty of pride," Tony assured him. "just not on the back of a horse." He winced as he shifted position in the saddle. "Not anymore, at least." He tipped his head to one side. "Looks like you kept riding even when you were in California."

"Oh, yeah." He and Julie had lived in Orange County, not exactly a horse-friendly place. Too much asphalt. Too many houses, cars and people. Since he'd missed the feel of being out in the open, just him and his mount, Cam had found a stable in Irvine Ranch that allowed him to board a horse and explore what had once been the largest privately held ranch in California.

Of course, the Irvine family had sold off huge sections of their holdings over the years, but there were still hills and valleys that were unspoiled and just right for what he'd needed.

But being back in Texas fed Cam's soul in a way he hadn't known he needed. With the afternoon sun blasting down on them from a clear blue sky, it was a picture-perfect Texas day, even if the heat would soon be murderous in the middle of summer.

Turning to look at Tony again, he asked, "What do you think of the property?"

The other man's gaze swept the meadow that was surrounded by oaks before shifting his gaze to Cam. "Honestly, it's perfect. Are you sure you want to do this?"

"Absolutely," Cam said, his voice firm enough to

convince his friend. “This section is far enough from the main house that your ‘campers’ won’t interfere with the ranch. And it’s close enough that I can ride down here when I get a need for some baseball.”

Tony grinned. “Still miss it, don’t you?”

“I do.” Nodding, he said, “In high school, I was sure you and I would go to college together, then get drafted by the same big-league team. I pictured us playing together for years.”

“Yeah, me too. The best fastball pitcher in Texas with the best damn catcher in the world.”

Cam laughed. “I was the best in Texas, but you got the world?”

Tony laughed, too, and Cam realized how much he’d missed this. Being with people he’d known his whole life. Being in the place where he’d grown up. Had roots. Connections.

“Long-term lease?” his friend asked.

“A hundred dollars a year for fifty years. How’s that sound?”

“Perfect,” Tony said. “Still don’t know why you want to do this, but I’m grateful.” He looked out at the land again and so did Cam. It was as if the two old friends were staring at what would soon be. The dugouts, the fields, the batting cages. The kids, shrieking, laughing, discovering a love for baseball.

With another sigh of satisfaction, Cam said, “I’ll call my lawyers. Get things moving.” He turned his horse's head toward home, then looked back at Tony, who hadn't moved.

"You coming?"

"That depends. Any chance you could send a jeep back to get me?"

"Not a single one," Cam told him with a grin.

"I figured," Tony said with a half groan. "The things I do for baseball."

Beth was waiting on the porch when Cam and Tony rode into the yard. A jolt of electricity seemed to hit him dead center of the chest and left him wondering if he would always react to her like that.

Taking the front steps down to the graveled drive, she waited for them, and in the sunlight her hair looked like gold. Her eyes were hidden behind a pair of oversize sunglasses, and her mouth was firmed into a straight line. She wore cream-colored slacks, an emerald green shirt with short sleeves and a high stand-up collar, and a pair of heeled sandals that displayed toes painted a bright purple. A slight wind lifted her hair off her shoulders and it shone like an aura around her head.

"Beth!" Tony said as he slid gracelessly from his horse. "What're you doing here?" He shot a look at Cam. "Are you two on again?"

"No," Beth said before Cam could do it. "Definitely not."

There was a bite in her voice that hadn't been

there before, and Cam gave her a curious glance. She ignored it.

"I'm just here to help him with some plans for his guest ranch."

"Uh-huh." Tony looked from one to the other of them, and the expression on his face said plainly that he didn't believe that for a second. Cam had always said Tony was a smart man.

Beth shook her head, walked a few steps and hugged Tony. "It's good to see you, though. What're you doing here?"

"Getting the land I need for my baseball camp," he said with a grateful nod at Cam.

"Really?" She looked at Cam, too, and he wished she'd take off the sunglasses so he could get an idea of what she was thinking, feeling. Instead, she kept those feelings hidden from him.

Cam shrugged. "It's a good deal for both of us."

"Better for me, not that I'm complaining." Tony hugged Beth again before letting her go.

It was a bitch to be jealous of your old friend embracing the woman you yourself wanted to be holding.

"But right now," Tony said, "I'm going to hobble home and get into the hot tub."

"Pitiful, man…"

Tony laughed. "Yeah, we'll see how you feel when I get you out on the pitcher's mound for the first time in years."

"Deal."

Once his friend was gone, Beth plucked her sunglasses off and looked up at Cam. He read the banked anger in those green depths made darker and greener by the shirt she wore.

"Let's get out of the sun," he said, and waved one arm toward the house. She hesitated briefly as if trying to decide if she should go in or not; finally she took the porch steps up to the front door and stepped inside.

Cam led her into the great room and watched her take it in. He hadn't been back long, but getting your house furnished quickly wasn't a problem if you were willing to pay for express delivery.

Chocolate leather couches and chairs were spread around the room. Heavy oak tables held brass lamps with cream shades, and the rugs on the wide-plank dark floor were in deep tones of red and gold. The stone fireplace took up most of one wall, and a big-screen TV held a place of honor on another. It was a man's room and he knew it. Most people would say it needed a woman's touch, but as far as Cam could tell, it was perfect just as it was.

"The house still needs some work. And I'm going to do some remodeling, but the structure's sound enough."

"Well, it is about one hundred years old, so a little work isn't out of line," she murmured.

"That's what I thought."

Beth turned to look at him. He noticed the anger was still there, glittering like shards of ice in the forest of her eyes.

"Remember how we used to make plans for this place?"

"I remember," she answered. "I remember we made a lot of plans back then."

"Yeah." He pulled off his hat, set it crown down on the closest table and ran his hands through his hair again. "We did."

"And now that you're back, you're making a heck of a statement. The donation to the hospital. Now Tony's baseball camp."

She didn't sound pleased by any of it. "Is it so hard to believe that I'm back to stay? That I want to be a part of Royal?"

"You left before, Cam," she said. "Why wouldn't you go again?"

"Because that's done. Because I *chose* to come home. Because it's where I want to be."

"Right." She nodded stiffly. Her shoulders were rigid, her chin lifted and her eyes were still bristling with emotions. "And I should take your word for that."

"What's going on, Beth?" His gaze locked with hers, and mentally he braced himself for whatever was coming. Clearly, it wasn't good.

"I went to see Burt Wheeler today."

That would explain the mood she was in. Burt

was a hard man to talk to under the best of circumstances. And since she'd been there on Cam's behalf, it couldn't have been easy.

"Yeah? How'd it go?"

She dropped her purse on a table and looked at him. "As you expected it to." She tucked her hair behind her ears, and her gold earrings glittered in the sunlight sliding in through the front windows. "He's not happy, but he'll put your name up for membership because it's his job. He just won't vote for you."

"More than I thought he'd do." Cam ran one hand across the back of his neck and then shoved both hands into his pockets. He didn't much like the idea of sending Beth to his father-in-law as a go-between. He usually handled his own business. His own problems. But he hadn't had much choice, either. Joining the TCC was elemental to any plans he was going to set into motion now that he was home. "Thanks. I know it wasn't easy."

"No, it wasn't," Beth admitted, then shrugged. "But it was our bargain, right?"

"Yeah." Nodding, Cam kept his gaze fixed on her because he had a feeling another shoe was about to drop. "But something tells me there's more chewing you up inside. So why don't you just say it, Beth?"

Beth felt his steady stare as she would have his hands on her body. He'd always had the ability to look at her as if he was seeing something deep inside of her. She'd felt at times that she couldn't keep a secret from him because somehow Cam would know. Apparently, though, he had no problem at all hiding truths he wanted locked away.

She'd been holding herself together ever since leaving Burt Wheeler's place. She'd smiled through lunch with Gracie, then made a few more donation stops before dropping her friend off at her home. It was only then she'd given her emotions full rein. Only then that she allowed herself to really think about what Burt had said.

Julie. Pregnant.

She looked up at the man standing in front of her and accepted that she'd been wrong about Cam fifteen years ago. She'd believed he'd never leave. And he had. She had believed he loved her—but he'd apparently been sleeping with Julie, too.

"Beth?" His voice was low, almost intimate, and that was what pushed her into blurting out the truth.

"Burt told me Julie was pregnant when the two of you ran away."

God. Fresh pain welled up and stung her eyes with tears she absolutely refused to shed. He'd betrayed her even more completely than she'd once believed. Just thinking about it now made her want to block everything from her mind so the pain would stop.

But she couldn't do that. She had to know. Staring up at Cam, she waited for him to say something. *Anything.* But his features were cold and hard. His dark brown eyes were shadowy places where the truth lay hidden.

Yet he didn't deny it. How could he?

Beth's heart ached more with every silent second that ticked past. As she watched him, she saw his eyes fill with sympathy. Regret. That told her everything she needed to know.

Shaking her head, she turned away from him until he finally spoke.

"I'm sorry, Beth. I should have thought that Burt would say something."

"Oh, God." She turned to him again and slapped one hand to her chest to try to ease the pain of her heart being squeezed by a giant cold fist. "Julie *was* pregnant."

"Yes."

One word. Clipped. No explanation. Then again, she ranted internally, how could there be? How could he possibly explain getting another girl pregnant while he was Beth's boyfriend?

"Thank you for that, anyway," she muttered.

"What?"

"For not denying it. For not lying to me. Again. My God, what an idiot I was." She choked out a laugh. "No wonder my father wanted to break us up. He knew I wasn't able to see you for who you really were."

"You did see me."

"Not then. But I do now."

"Damn it, Beth..." Cam stood there, hands at his sides, looking into her eyes as if willing her to give him a chance to explain. But what could he say? And why should she listen?

"No. There's nothing you can say that makes this all right," she murmured.

"I'm not going to try to explain. You wouldn't believe me anyway," he said, and irritation was clear in his tone. "Your mind is set on one thing, and you don't want to see the other side."

"What possible other side is there?" she demanded.

He scrubbed one hand across his jaw and shook his head grimly. "You're too emotional about this to hear me out."

Beth's eyes went wide and she actually felt her jaw drop. "Seriously?" she asked, stunned. "I'm too emotional? So I'm the bad guy here?"

"Who said there has to be a bad guy?" His demand rang out in the otherwise still room and seemed to hang in the air.

Beth stared at him as if she'd never seen him before. And maybe she hadn't. Not really. As a kid, she'd seen him through rainbows and flowers. Since he'd come back home, she'd seen him through the fog of memory and maybe it was only now that she was seeing Camden for who he actually was. It broke her heart.

"One of us cheated on the other one," Beth said,

and gave herself points for keeping a check on the rage inside. "One of us got someone pregnant." She whirled around, took three quick steps toward the stone fireplace on the far wall, then spun back again to face him. "There is no other side to this, Cam. I was your girlfriend and the girl you *married* was pregnant."

A single tear escaped and Beth swiped it away hurriedly, hoping to hell he hadn't seen it. She wasn't going to give him her tears again. God knew she'd cried oceans of them all those years ago.

Cam pushed both hands through his hair, then let them fall. It was more than regret in his eyes now. There was surprise, as well. And anger. "How can you think I cheated on you?"

Wide eyed, she stared at him. "How can I not? You married Julie. She was pregnant. What else am I supposed to think?"

His features were grim as he watched her, and Beth would have given anything to know what he was thinking. Were his thoughts racing, trying to find a way out of this? Trying to somehow make having a child with another woman a happy thing? That thought prompted her next question.

"And while we're on the subject," she added, lifting her chin and locking her gaze with his. "Where is your child? Should be almost fifteen, right? Boy or girl?"

The muscle in Cam's jaw twitched as if he were

chewing over what he wanted to say. Finally he simply said, “Julie lost the baby when she was five months pregnant.”

That stopped her for a moment. He’d cheated on her. Beth remembered the never ending wave of pain at being so completely discarded that the echoes of it could make her chest hurt. But she wouldn’t have wished his child gone. “I’m sorry, Cam.”

His gaze flicked to hers, and his eyes went cool and distant in a second.

“I’m not talking about this with you,” he muttered. “Not now.”

She laughed and the sound scraped across her throat. “Not then and not now. Perfect. That’s great. You didn’t tell me you were leaving and now that you’re back, you won’t tell me why any of it happened. Fantastic.”

Beth grabbed her purse and slung the slender gold chain strap over her shoulder. “Enjoy the TCC membership, Camden.”

When she stalked past him, he reached for her, but she pulled her arm away before he could grab hold. “No. You don’t get to do that. Touch me as if we still have something between us.”

“There will *always* be something between us, Beth.” His voice was so low she could hardly hear it. And maybe that was just as well. She was trembling, hurting and so furious at her own gullibility that she could hardly see.

"No, Camden. That ended a long time ago. When you betrayed me."

"Oh, no," he countered. "I'm willing to stand here and take everything else you said to me because I figure you've got a right. But you don't get to say I betrayed you."

Beth nodded jerkily. "Right. I forgot. *You're* the injured party here."

He didn't rise to that bait. Instead, he said simply, "You tore my heart out."

She pushed her hair back. "And you stomped on mine. Do we call it a tie?"

"We call it over." His eyes never left hers. His features were tight and his voice a deep whisper when he said, "It's done, Beth. Fifteen years done."

Her breaths were short and fast. Her heart was beating ferociously, and she told herself to get a grip. How could he stand there so calmly? She felt as if she were going to explode, but she couldn't as long as he was being so damn reasonable.

She wouldn't give him the satisfaction of seeing just how he could still affect her. Stiffly she nodded, though it cost her. How could she look into his eyes and want him so much it made her ache—in spite of their past?

Was he right about calling the past done and over? Could she leave it where it belonged and move forward? How could she if she couldn't trust him?

"And what are you suggesting?" she asked, suddenly tired and sure that her wildly swinging emotions were to blame for that. "We start over?"

He sighed, tipped his head back and stared at the ceiling for a slow count of three. Then he looked at her again. "We're not starting anything up, right? We're just going to learn to deal with living near each other again. That was the deal."

"Yeah, we're full of deals," Beth murmured darkly. She hated it, but he was right. They weren't starting anything. They weren't a couple any more than she and Justin were. And a part of her ached with that knowledge. "Fine. We go from here. Not friends. Not lovers. Just…what, exactly?"

"Hell if I know."

She laughed again and this time it was a little less painful. "That, at least, is honest."

"I didn't lie to you."

Beth held up one hand. "I don't want to talk about it." Taking a breath, she reached for something—anything to get them off the subject of their past. "You wanted to show me what you had in mind for your guest cottages, right?"

"Yeah," he said, keeping a wary eye on her as if half-waiting for her to explode again. "The plans are in the dining room."

"Great." Better than great. This gave her something to do. Something to think about besides a pregnant Julie and a cheating Cam. She followed him across the foyer to the formal dining room.

There was some truly hideous red-and-black-flocked wallpaper, but the space was huge and boasted windows on both walls. At the moment, the drapes were drawn as if Cam didn't want anyone else to have to see that wallpaper.

A huge reclaimed pine table sat in the center of the room and had ten chairs pulled up to it. The light fixture over the table was brass, with long arms and clear glass light globes attached to the ends.

Architect renderings and blueprints were scattered across the table, and Beth had to wonder why he needed her. At a glance she saw he had the layout of the cabins well planned.

"It looks like you've already got things set," she said, and took a closer look at the first sketch of a would-be cabin.

"They're bare-bones and—no offense to the LA architect—pretty cookie-cutter." He sighed. "I had these drawn up a year ago."

Surprise flickered through her. She shifted her gaze to him. "You've been planning to come back for a while, then."

He nodded. "It's been on my mind for a few years now. Having these done made it seem more real. Immediate. Most of the new developments out in California look like they've been stamped out on an assembly line, so that's what they design."

She half-laughed. "You really didn't like California."

He looked at her thoughtfully. "It's really not that bad. Its main problem for me was that it wasn't Texas. I wanted to be here. Now that I am, I want something different. I want the cabins to look like they *belong* there. A part of the ranch itself."

"Yeah, you said that." Idly Beth picked up a pencil and sketched a porch on one of the cabin drawings, then added window boxes and rockers on the porch. She had never been much of an artist, but it didn't look too bad to her eye. "Better?"

"Yes." He smiled at her, and her breath caught.

She didn't want to feel for him. Didn't want to be drawn to him. But it seemed what she wanted and what was happening were two separate things.

"You can make each cabin different by adding little finishes or even by differing the structures themselves. Arched doorways, painted different colors." She lifted one shoulder in a shrug. "Log cabins, Victorians, bungalows, hobbit houses. Give them each a personality."

"You're good at this," he mused.

His voice was too soft. He was standing too close. He smelled too good. Beth had come here riding on fury, but that had passed, leaving her feeling hollowed out. She still didn't have answers, but what she did have, as always, was this driving need for Camden Guthrie.

"I should go," she said.

"Don't."

Looking up into his eyes, she fought with herself internally. Beth knew she should leave, but her feet wouldn't move. She knew that if she stayed, nothing would be resolved. It was more likely the problems and mistrust between them would only grow. Sex wasn't in itself an answer and often just led to muddying things up even more.

"You're looking at me like you're trying to solve a mystery."

"Maybe I am," she admitted.

"It's just not that complicated, Beth."

"Please." She shook her head and nearly smiled. "You've always been complicated, Camden."

"There you're wrong," he said, moving in a little closer so that she couldn't breathe without taking his scent inside her. "When it came to you, I wasn't complicated at all."

She sighed, still trying to stop what was inevitably crashing toward her. "Until you left with another woman."

"You don't understand, Beth," he said. "Any of it."

"Then explain it to me. After all these years, *tell* me."

He frowned. "We open this door—there's no going back."

"Maybe there shouldn't be," Beth said, even knowing that what she might hear could tear her heart to pieces. "We keep twisting the doorknob, but we never open it. Never look. Isn't it better to *know* the truth?"

He studied her, and emotions darted across the surface of his eyes so quickly she couldn't have named them all.

Maybe she was crazy to open this all up now. Maybe it would be better if she never knew what had happened so long ago. But if she didn't take this step, her dreams would always be tortured. She would always wonder how he could have chosen Julie over her.

Keeping her gaze locked with his, she asked, "Julie was pregnant. Were you cheating on me the whole time? Were you and Julie laughing at me?"

"What? *No.*" He turned and kicked the wall, then whipped back around to face her. "How could you think that?"

"How could I not?" she countered. "We were together for three years and then suddenly you and Julie run away to get married? What the hell, Camden?"

"We're just going to jump right in, huh? Fine." He took a step closer. "Like you said, we were together three years. We had plans, too, Beth. Or did you forget all about them that last night we were together when you shot it all down and tossed us aside? Tossed *me* aside?"

"I didn't do that."

"The hell you didn't." His voice was tight and

low and thrumming with the same anger she felt. "Instead of getting married and going off to college together, you said you needed 'time.' That you were too young all of a damn sudden. *We* were too young."

She remembered it all as clearly as he did. "We were, Cam. I was only eighteen."

"Didn't bother you before that night. What the hell changed?" The challenge was clear in his tone. "Was it your father? He hated you being with an 'Indian.'"

"You're wrong." Beth shook her head firmly. "He didn't care about that. What he cared about was that you had no money. No prospects. He wanted us to wait. Was that really so wrong?"

"No, what was wrong was you parroting everything your old man said and then acting like it was your version of the truth."

Beth took a deep breath and blinked frantically to hold back tears of frustration. "All I said was I wanted to wait. To take some time apart to make sure."

"Translation—" he bit off. "We're done."

"No. You're wrong." She stormed closer, too, and poked his chest with her index finger. "That may be what you heard, but I never said I didn't want you. God help me," she admitted, her voice dropping. "Even after everything that's happened I *still* want you."

Seven

Cam grabbed her as they'd both known he would.

He pulled her in close, kissed her senseless, then lifted his head and stared down into her eyes. Beth got lost there, as she always had. It didn't matter what else was going on. This amazing, nearly magical feeling of being held by him would always drive her. She'd missed him so much. Missed *them* so much that now that he was holding her again, she could think of nothing else.

Her mouth was buzzing from that kiss, her blood bubbling in her veins, and all she could see was him. Maybe this had been unavoidable after all. This slow slide into Camden's arms.

Staring into his eyes, she whispered, “This solves nothing.”

“Maybe it doesn’t have to,” he said softly, his gaze moving over her face as if he’d hungered for no more than simply seeing her again.

“Maybe not,” she agreed as her heart began to race. “No more talking.”

“None,” he muttered, and kissed her again. His mouth ravaged hers, taking, giving, demanding. She was breathless as his lips, teeth and tongue claimed every inch of her mouth and silently demanded more.

He scraped his hands up and down her back, and all she could think was that she had too many clothes on. She needed to feel his hands on her skin.

As if he’d heard that stray thought, Cam tore his mouth from hers and looked down into her eyes as he tugged the hem of her shirt free of her slacks. Sliding one hand beneath the cool green fabric, he skimmed his fingertips across her abdomen and then up to cup her breast, and even through the fragile lace, she felt the heat of him.

His thumb and forefinger tweaked at her nipple and a shiver swept over her. Need erupted and she moaned softly, arching into him, pushing her breast into his hand, wishing her bra off and away. Then he took care of that, too. He flicked open the closure between her breasts and then he was touching her. Skin to skin, the heat overwhelming.

Beth stared up at him and saw her past, her present, her future, staring back at her. For her it had always been Camden. And maybe it always would be.

"Gotta get this off," he murmured, shifting his hold on her so he could work on the tiny buttons lining the front of her shirt. "Have to touch you. Feel you."

"Yes." She watched his strong hands and nimble fingers make short work of the buttons, then shrugged out of the shirt and tossed it onto the table as soon as he was finished. He slid her bra straps down her shoulders and let the pale blue lace drop to the floor.

"You're even more beautiful than I remembered," he whispered, and bent his head to take first one hardened nipple then the other into his mouth.

A groan erupted from her throat. She tipped her head back and stared unseeing at the ceiling. Her knees were weak, but Cam had one arm hooked around her waist holding her up as his mouth did incredible things to her body. His lips and tongue pulled at her nipples. The edges of his teeth scraped the tender flesh, and when he suckled her she felt the pull all the way down to her toes. She held on to his shoulders, digging her fingers into the fabric of his white shirt and the whipcord muscles beneath it.

When he dropped his free hand to the clasp of her slacks, then dipped his fingers beneath the elastic band of her panties to drive deeply into her heat, Beth exploded with an orgasm so shattering it stole her breath. She hadn't meant to come so quickly. Hadn't expected to. But her body had been starved for him for so long that his barest touch had driven her over the edge.

He held her while she trembled and rode the wave of the sensations claiming her. When she finally drew a breath again, she looked up into his eyes and found hunger stamped there so blatantly she almost came again.

"Upstairs," he said tightly.

"Yes," Beth answered. "Quickly."

"You read my mind," he admitted. Grabbing her shirt off the table, he swung her into his arms and headed for the stairs.

"I can walk," she told him, looking up into the harsh, taut planes of his face as he took the stairs two at a time.

"Not fast enough." He kept his gaze fixed ahead and she watched him, feeling her stomach swirl with the overwhelming reactions he caused in her. Seeing the blatant need on his features only inflamed her own.

Beth tore at the buttons on his shirt, and when two of them popped free she slid one hand across his chest as he made a left turn at the landing. He hissed in a breath at her touch and she smiled, knowing that she affected him as strongly as he did her.

Her fingers defined his hard, muscled chest, and all she could think was she wanted to be lying on top of him. To feel their bodies pressed together. Then he stalked into a room at the end of the hall and Beth took a quick look around.

The huge square room was as deliberately masculine as the great room downstairs. A massive four poster bed covered in a bloodred duvet took dominance and, frankly, was the only piece of furniture she was interested in at the moment. And still, she noticed the two chairs pulled up in front of a brick fireplace. The dressers, the bookcases, and the flat screen television on the wall facing the bed.

Then her mental tour was over as Cam dropped her onto the mattress and stood looking down at her. He wasted no time tearing his shirt off and tossing it aside. Beth kicked off her heeled sandals and squirmed out of her slacks and panties, all the while watching Camden remove his boots and jeans. And when he was standing beside the bed naked, she took a moment to just enjoy the view.

His body was hard and muscled, speaking more of years of hard work than a gym. As he stared down at her, she saw his eyes flash with the same raw desire peaking inside her. Gazes locked, he reached into the bedside table drawer, pulled out a condom and, ripping it open, sheathed himself in seconds. Then he moved so quickly she hardly saw the action. He caught her legs in his hands and pulled her to the edge of the mattress.

"Camden..."

"We agreed," he reminded her. "No more talking."

"Yes, but—"

He knelt before her and lowered his mouth to her center. Instantly, talking was the last thing on Beth's mind. She gasped at the sensation of his mouth and tongue working her most sensitive flesh. Again and again, he licked at her, suckling at the center bud until Beth thought she would lose her mind. She tried to twist and writhe on the bed to ease the ache, the tingles of expectation building inexorably inside, but Cam held her fast to the bed. She was caught in his grasp, and there was nowhere else she wanted to be.

The only sound was the soft purr of the air conditioner. The duvet beneath her felt cool and silky on her skin. Her breath wheezed in and out of her lungs as Camden drove her quietly insane.

His hot breath brushed against her as his tongue stroked her into a frenzy of need so wild it made that first shattering orgasm feel insignificant in comparison. He took her to the very brink of explosion time and again and, each time, pulled her back before allowing her to fall.

She reached down, threaded her fingers through his hair and tugged, making him look at her, making him see what he was doing to her. "Don't stop, Camden."

"Need to be inside you," he muttered, and this time when he pushed her to the very edge of oblivion, he pulled away, shifted her on the bed and then covered her body with his.

This was what she'd craved, Beth thought wildly. This melding of bodies, this press of his flesh to hers. The feel of his heart pounding against hers. And when he drove his body into hers, Beth lifted both of her legs, wrapping them around his hips as she tried to take him more deeply.

His body pounded into hers and she rocked with him, riding the rhythm he set, breathless as she scored his back with her fingernails. She tucked her face into the curve of his neck and bit him as the first explosion roared through her.

He groaned and pumped faster, harder, driving them both in their frenzy to finally at long last feel the crash of release they both needed so badly. Her insides coiled, tighter, tighter, building toward something earth-shattering. Cam raised his head and she shifted to take his mouth, to tangle her tongue with his, to draw his breath into her lungs and give him hers.

But when her climax hit her with the force of a hundred orgasms at once, Beth pulled her mouth free and screamed out his name. Head back, eyes wide, she felt herself splinter into a million pieces and didn't care. Tremors rattled her body as he drove her on and on, never stopping.

Beth wrapped her arms around his neck and held on to him as the only stable point in her suddenly spinning universe. She was still clinging to him when Cam's body exploded into hers, and together they took that fall.

A few minutes later, Cam was still trying to catch his breath. With Beth tucked into his side, he stared up at the beamed ceiling and fought his own internal struggle. Being with Beth again had soothed corners of his soul that he hadn't even realized had been ragged and worn.

And he didn't feel even slightly guilty about that. Which made him feel a pang of guilt. Hell, he'd been *married* to a woman he'd come to love, and he'd never once experienced anything like what he'd just survived with Beth. His heart was still racing and his dick was ready to go again—in spite of what his mind was currently torturing him with.

"Camden?"

He blew out a breath and turned his head to look at her. Beth's hair was a tangle of gold, and her green eyes shone in the afternoon light. Her mouth was bruised and puffy, and she had one leg hooked across him.

All he wanted was to gather her up and have her again. To feel that magical moment when his body became a part of hers. But as they'd already discovered, that wouldn't solve anything.

"That was..."

"Yeah, it was," he said, and shifted, going up on one elbow to look down at her.

She pushed a hand through her hair, swiping it back from her face. Afternoon sunlight drifted through the windows, slanting across the bed, throwing her eyes into shadow. He used to be fascinated by her eyes, Cam thought. Everything she felt was reflected there. He always knew what she was thinking because her eyes kept no secrets.

But now she guarded her mysteries. There was a wall between them now—and a part of him was grateful for it.

Their connection was fragile and it should probably stay that way. He wasn't looking for the kind of relationship with Beth that he'd once dreamed of. Today they were different people. The fact that the heat between them had only intensified didn't change a damn thing. In fact, it complicated things further.

"You don't have to get that look on your face," Beth warned.

"What look?"

"The one that clearly reads, *How close is the nearest exit*?"

He scowled at her. "Think you know me so well, do you?"

"Absolutely," she said, then tipped her head to one side. "Tell me I'm wrong."

"You're wrong. That's not what I was thinking at all."

"Great," she said. "Then what?"

"Just that this doesn't—"

"Matter? I know. We both knew that going in, didn't we?"

All he could do was stare at her. Why was she being so damn reasonable? Where was her fury from earlier? Was she really so able to compartmentalize this and tuck it away into the back of her mind? He had been prepared to pull back, to explain that they couldn't go forward from here. Now that she'd done it for him, Cam wasn't sure what to say.

"Relax, Camden." Beth scooted up higher on the pillows banked behind them. "I don't want anything from you."

That was a little insulting. "Why the hell not?"

"Because when I needed you, you left." She shrugged. "Why would I make the same mistake all over again?"

A punch to the gut would have been easier to take. "Are we back to that, then?"

"We never left it. There are too many unanswered questions hanging in the air between us, Cam."

"You want answers?" He'd kept his mouth shut about what had happened fifteen years ago. He'd never talked about it and had rarely thought about it once his decision to marry Julie had been made. Seemed like the time had come.

"You want answers?" he repeated. "Fine. Here's one. Up to you if you believe it or not."

She watched him through suspicious eyes. "Go ahead."

"Burt was right. Julie was pregnant when we got married."

"Yeah, thanks. I know that part." She pulled the edge of the duvet up and over her as if it were a shield.

"What you don't know is the baby wasn't mine." He'd never said those words out loud before. Cam rubbed the center of his chest, aware that it felt as though a heavy weight had suddenly been lifted off of him.

Her brow furrowed, and she looked at him as if he were speaking a foreign language. "What? Why? Who? Why did you marry her if it wasn't your baby? Who was the father?"

"That I won't tell you," he said firmly with a shake of his head. "It was Julie's secret to share or not."

She huffed out an exasperated breath. "You just expect me to take your word for it?"

"I told you. Believe it or not, that's up to you." He locked his gaze with hers. "But ask yourself. Why the hell would I lie?"

Beth glared at him. "I've got better questions. Why would you leave me and marry her, knowing she was carrying someone else's baby?"

He felt the scowl on his face and worked to ease it. Hadn't he just told her that this was all fifteen years gone? Wasn't it time to get it out there?

"After you and I split up—" When she opened her mouth to argue the point, he held up one hand. "Just let me tell it."

"Fine." She folded her arms over her chest, and he saw the defensive gleam in her eyes.

"I found Julie crying the next day." He closed his eyes briefly, remembering. "Sobbing like her heart was broken, and I guess it was. Anyway, I knew how she felt."

Beth's mouth worked as if she were biting back words clamoring to get out.

"She was pregnant and terrified to tell her father. Hell," he said grimly. "You know Burt. Can you imagine how he'd have taken that news?"

She nodded. "About as well as my father would have."

"Exactly. She said the baby's father was pushing her to marry him. He had plans for his own future, and that included getting a rich girl pregnant so he could worm his way into her family and bank accounts. Julie wouldn't marry him once she found that out. And she couldn't bear the thought of an abortion. Giving the baby up wasn't an option, either, because she had nowhere to go until she had the baby. She didn't know what to do. Asked me to help her. So I did."

"And getting married was your big solution?"

"Got me out of Royal," he said bluntly. "Away from you."

Beth choked out a laugh, slid off the bed and grabbed his white shirt off the floor. Pulling it on, the hem of the thing hit her midthigh, and rather than making her look more covered, Cam thought it only made her sexier.

"You had to get away from me."

"Yeah." He got up, too, and didn't bother to grab clothes. What was the point? "We were over and I couldn't stay here to watch you hook up with someone new."

"We weren't *done*."

"As far as I was concerned we were."

She shook her hair back from her face, and that long, blond tangle made him want to thread his fingers through it. He wanted her again. Always. And that was damned lowering.

"Then Julie lost the baby."

"Yeah."

"Why didn't you divorce, then? The reason for the marriage was over. You could have come back. Come home."

To me was left unsaid, but it felt like those two words were hanging in the air like a neon sign.

"Because we were married. I promised to stay with her." He rubbed one hand against the back of his neck. "And I did. But there were…complications with the miscarriage and Julie needed an emergency hysterectomy."

"Oh, God…"

Nodding, he just looked at her as he finished, "I couldn't leave her then. And by that time, I knew I couldn't come back here. You weren't mine anymore, and I knew you'd never understand what I did anyway..."

"You were right about that," she said. "I still don't."

He nodded. "Yeah, I get that. But you wanted the truth and now you have it. What're we going to do with it?"

"I don't know," Beth admitted hoarsely. She held the edges of his shirt together with a fist in the center of her chest.

Another defensive move?

Everything in him urged him to tumble her back onto the bed, where they could work out whatever problems they had in the one way that had always worked for them. But he didn't. Because sex—even spectacular sex—couldn't build the bridge they needed between them.

For years he'd been a husband. He hadn't cheated. He'd been loyal and had eventually come to love his wife.

It was different than what he had had with Beth, but no less important. Still, now that he'd been with Beth again, he could admit that he was finally letting Julie go. And that bothered him enough that his voice sounded colder than he might have intended.

"I can't tell you what's coming. Who the hell

could?" Irritation clawed at his throat and fought with the desire already pulsing inside him again. "All I know is I want you. Always have. Always will. What we do with that…"

"Right." Beth took a deep breath and lifted her chin when she looked at him. "I might never be okay with what you did."

"I didn't ask you to be," he reminded her.

"I can't trust you," she said.

That slammed into him, and he didn't like the feel of it at all. "I didn't betray you."

"From your perspective."

"That's the only one I've got."

She smiled briefly, and even that slight curve of her mouth sent a charge through Cam's system that almost stole his breath. How had he forgotten what it was like to touch her? To be inside her? Had he deliberately forgotten so that he could survive the years without her? Whatever the reason, it didn't matter now. She was here. With him. The long time without her had only made the hunger that much more overpowering.

"Anyway," Beth continued as if he hadn't spoken. She walked around the end of the bed and stopped just a foot or so in front of him. A slash of sunlight bathed her in a soft golden glow that made her shine even more than she usually did.

"You said it yourself. That was fifteen years ago." Her gaze locked with his, and in the shadows of her eyes he read a fire that they'd rekindled only minutes ago. "We're not kids now, Camden," she whispered. "And I don't believe in hearts and flowers and happily-ever-afters anymore."

She said it so simply that he believed her, and he hated it. Cam had always loved Beth's ability to believe in good things. To see the best in everything and rush to meet it. Until that last night.

"What I do believe in is what happens when I'm with you," she said. "And I want to feel it again. Now."

Cam didn't see a future for them, either. Hell, maybe a part of him had never believed in it. He was the son of a couple of horse trainers. He was the poor son of ranch hands and she was a damn princess—or as close to it as Royal could get. When that night had happened, he'd been crushed, but a silent, observant voice in his head had whispered, *There it is.* The end. Just like you thought it would be.

And really? What had changed? She was still out of his reach. But they did have the present and maybe they'd spent enough of it talking. Without another word between them, he hauled her in close, kissed her until he thought he'd die from it and then whipped up the hem of the shirt covering her.

Her hands moved over his bare back, nails scraping, leaving marks as if branding him, and he was okay with it. As long as she was in his arms, he'd figure out the rest. He lifted her off her feet, and she wrapped her legs around his hips as he spun to brace her back against the nearest wall.

They crashed into it, both of them losing their breath but not their will to join. To be locked together. He looked into her eyes as he pushed himself into her heat, and he saw the flare of wild need electrify her eyes.

She kissed him then and tangled her tongue with his. Her breath slid into his lungs, and he let her fill him as he filled her. His hands at her hips, he held her as he rocked in and out of her body, giving himself up to the fire within. Again and again he claimed her, took her, giving as much as he got. Needing her more with every passing second.

He felt her body tighten. Felt the first stir of completion when it took her and he gave her more, pushed her higher, faster than he had before, and when she tore her mouth from his to shout his name at the ceiling, he felt her body convulse around his.

Cam watched her face as she came and realized he'd never seen anything more beautiful. She was what had been missing from his life. And for this moment at least, she was back. She was his. He was hers. For this one stolen piece of time, there was no past, no future. Only the now.

And when his own body shattered, he felt his soul go with it.

Eight

By the following afternoon, Beth was in the middle of the Fire Department Open House and watching the money add up in the giant glass barrel she'd set on the catering table.

They'd already collected enough money through donations and the sale of raffle tickets to fulfill the fire station's wish list for new equipment. But these last-minute donations, given by the people stopping to pick up sandwiches, ice-cream bars and soda or water, were creating a nice bonus. And it was fun, watching the bills and change in the barrel mount up.

This half of Main Street had been blocked off by Nathan Battles and his deputies, allowing people to stream back and forth across the street without keeping an eye out for cars. The crowd was huge, but then Beth had counted on that. People in Royal could be depended on to show up for a good cause—and keeping their own fire station well equipped served all of them.

Her whole family was there, and she grinned to see Piper out on the dance floor with old Mr. Martin as he led her in a slow, dignified Texas-style waltz. Piper caught her eye and smiled back, just before the country and western band switched it up from slow to fast and new dancers took the stage.

"This is amazing," Gracie said, and had to lean in close to Beth's ear just to be heard over the band.

"Turned out great, didn't it?" Beth looked around at the size of the crowd and then noticed Justin heading toward her.

She didn't need to deal with this today. Especially after yesterday and those amazing, soul shattering hours with Camden. God. She should be regretting the decision she'd made to sleep with Cam, but how could she? She'd never known anything like what she experienced with him. But how could she trust him? How could she ever hope for them to be more than simply lovers?

In spite of what she'd told him the day before, she *did* believe in love and marriage and the happily-ever-after that had eluded her so far. Once she'd thought that future would include Cam; now she didn't see how it could.

Still, that didn't mean her future would include Justin.

Beth turned and told Gracie, "Gotta get lost in the crowd. Justin's coming and I just can't do this today."

Gracie looked past her and said, "Go. I'll stall him."

"Remind me to give you a raise."

"I will." Gracie smiled and went to head Justin off.

Beth, meanwhile, slipped into the crowd, ducking behind people, hoping to lose herself. She caught snatches of conversation, eruptions of laughter and squeals from little kids. It was all so normal. Except for what she was up to. Imagine being a grown woman and hiding from a man rather than just telling him to go away.

But, in her defense, Justin didn't *listen.*

"What are you doing?"

She looked up and grimaced at her cousin Zeke. "Hiding. Don't give me away."

Zeke turned to look in the direction she'd come from and sighed. "Can't he take a hint?"

"Apparently not." She looked up at him and pleaded, "Help."

"Right." He grabbed her hand, pulled her onto the dance floor behind him and barely slowed down when she squawked.

"This is *not* hiding, Zeke."

"No, this is dancing." He slipped his arm around her, took her right hand in his and smoothly moved them in with the other dancers. "Don't worry, I won't let him cut in."

"You'd better not." After a second or two, she looked up at him and asked, "Don't you have someone here you'd rather be dancing with than your cousin?"

"Not at the moment," he confessed, then grinned at her. "Besides, I dance with my cousin, and I look like a great guy to all the interesting women around here."

She laughed. "So you're using me."

"Absolutely." He winked and spun her into a turn.

The crowd was a mash of color and movement. The music was loud but catchy, and the local band knew exactly the kind of songs to play to keep their audience dancing. This was Texas, so the music was country, but the beat was so good that even those who preferred rock and roll were kept happy enough.

"You did a great job on this, Beth."

"Thanks." She looked to her right. On the other side of the fire station, the gleaming red-and-white trucks sat in the sun while children climbed all over them. "I think we pulled it off."

"I'll say. Did you see Bob Hackett when he won that truck?" Zeke laughed. "I thought his eyes were going to bug out of his head."

"Well, he's twenty-two and just got a brand-new top-of-the-line truck. That's enough to make anybody a little bug-eyed."

"Yeah, he's posing for pictures with it. I think his girlfriend, Cherry, is getting jealous. He keeps touching that truck like he's afraid it's going to disappear."

Beth knew that feeling. She'd had it yesterday when she couldn't stop touching Camden—a stroke on his arm, a caress across his chest, smoothing his hair back from his forehead. It was as if she had to keep feeling him to reassure herself that he was really there. With her. After so long without him, having him close again had been almost dreamlike.

"Oh, God."

"What?" Zeke looked at her, startled. "What's wrong?"

"Nothing. Just…nothing." She kept dancing and told herself that she was wrong. She couldn't possibly still be in love with Camden Guthrie. Not after everything that had happened. Not after he'd betrayed her, left town, married Julie Wheeler.

And she realized that, no, she wasn't *still* in love with him. This love was new. It was based on who he was now.

Yes, he was basically the same man he'd been back in the day. But now he was self-assured. Comfortable in his own skin and making no apologies for what he wanted. Then there was helping Tony out with the baseball camp. Him hiring Olivia Turner and her crew of mostly female construction experts. He had made a huge donation to the children's wing.

Hell, even the loyalty he'd shown the woman he'd

left Beth for had made an impact on her. He was touching her heart again, and he was making plans for a future here. In Royal.

Of course she was in love with him again. She'd been predisposed for the fall. They shared a past that was taut with both pain and joy, and now that he was home the future dangled out in front of her like a shiny prize she just couldn't reach.

"Seriously, Beth," Zeke said. "You okay? You look a little pale."

"I'm just hot." Big lie since the wide Texas sky was studded with massive white clouds that kept playing tag across the sun, keeping the heat to a minimum. But her cousin accepted it because he was a good guy.

"Beth—" Gracie rushed across the dance floor. "I tried, but Justin's on his way over here, so—"

"Thanks for the heads-up." She looked up at Zeke. "Sorry."

"No problem." He gave her a grin that made his green eyes shine. "I'll just sweep Gracie off her feet."

"Oh, you don't have—"

Beth laughed as Gracie's refusal was lost in the dance. Zeke swung her into a country swing dance, and Beth left as Gracie was spinning and laughing up at her partner.

It wasn't as if Beth could leave the party—she was in charge of it. But she didn't want to talk to Justin. She stopped to chat with her neighbors, waved to friends as she passed and checked in with the firefighters. Some were giving tours of the station house, and others were riding herd on a dozen kids crawling all over the gleaming red fire truck as well as the EMS truck.

Smiling, Beth told herself to just concentrate on the day. To push all thoughts of Cam and whatever they were to each other to the back of her mind. It wasn't as if she could solve anything right now anyway. And as if the Fates were laughing, Cam stepped up behind her.

"You look beautiful."

She turned at the sound of that deep voice and looked up into chocolate eyes that were burning with the same kind of intensity she'd seen the day before. Her entire body snapped with the sizzle suddenly bubbling in her blood.

"Thank you." She wore a sky blue dress with shoulder straps, a squared neckline and a full skirt. Her favorite heeled sandals completed the outfit and brought her much closer to eye level with the man currently staring at her as if he could gulp her up.

She gave Cam a quick once-over and nearly sighed. His gray Stetson was pulled low over his eyes. He wore a white dress shirt, a black blazer and black jeans with a pair of polished black boots that completed the image of "dangerous cowboy." And that's just what he was.

"What're you doing here?" she asked.

He shrugged and looked out over the crowd. "I live here, Beth. I ought to be part of the town." He shifted his gaze back to hers. "And I figured it was a good place to run into you."

When her heart did a ridiculous flip, she told herself to just stop it. Unfortunately, her body wasn't listening to her head.

"Beth?" Another deep voice, easier to hear this far from the band's speakers.

She turned and smiled as James Harris stepped up to give her a quick hug. James was tall and gorgeous, with closely cropped black hair, dark brown eyes and skin the color of melted caramel.

"James, hi."

"You did a great job with this event," he said. "Makes me really look forward to the party at the TCC this October. Can't wait to see what you'll come up with for that."

"Oh," she said, smiling, "you're going to love it. I've got lots of plans."

He laughed. "I'll bet." Then he shifted a glance at Cam. "Hey, Camden. Good to have you back in Royal." He held out one hand and Cam shook it, smiling.

"Good to be back. I've been thinking about coming to see you. The word is you breed the best horses in East Texas."

"I'll agree with that," James said with a grin.

"Well, I'm going to be needing a couple dozen

horses out at my place. I figure you're the man to see."

"Great. I can set you up." James was the top horse breeder in the county, and people came from all over the West to buy his horses. "Come out anytime, look them over and we'll do a deal." He paused then said, "Meanwhile, I talked to Burt Wheeler the other day."

Beth winced and Cam's features tightened. Neither of them were certain what he'd heard from Burt.

"Yeah, he's not my biggest fan."

"He did make that pretty clear," James confirmed, and let it lie, thank goodness. "But he did say you're interested in joining the TCC."

"I am," Cam said. "And I hear you're the president now."

"Guilty as charged," James replied with another grin. "Anyway, wanted to let you know that I don't see a problem with your membership at all. Burt might not be happy about it, but I'm looking forward to welcoming you all the way home."

Cam's features cleared, and Beth could almost see tension drain out of his body. "Thanks, James. I appreciate it."

"Not a problem. It'll be good to have you as a member." He hugged Beth again and said, "Now, I'm off to find a beer. You guys have fun."

"Well," Cam murmured, "that's one worry off the table."

"I'm glad for you," she said, and found she meant

it. It was another tie to Royal. Another thing to keep him here, and that was more important to Beth than she would have thought.

The music changed again and this time it was perfect for a two-step. Beth tapped her foot in time and Cam must have noticed.

"The band's good. You want to see if we've still got it?"

She looked up at him and, damn it, *smiled.* The two-step had always been *their* dance. They'd even won a couple of contests as kids. "It's been a long time."

"Like riding a horse, darlin'," he assured her, and took her hand, leading her to the wooden dance floor erected for the party.

They took a spot in the crowd. Cam's right hand was positioned behind her left shoulder, and Beth rested her left arm atop his. His Stetson shaded his eyes, but she saw the shine there anyway and bubbles of pleasure raced through her. A couple of years ago, she never would have guessed that she and Cam would be dancing together again.

And then they were moving, sliding into the steps as if they'd never been apart. He was smooth and easy to follow. Their steps were quick, then slow, and they seemed to glide together effortlessly. When he spun her around she swayed with the movement, then right back again. They moved around the dance floor, part of the crowd yet separate. Their eyes locked and the years fell away.

In a blink, Beth remembered all the nights by the lake with the car radio blasting so they could practice their steps. And she remembered how those practice sessions had always ended in the back seat of her car—or his. Passion-fogged windows had encapsulated them in their own private world as they lost themselves in each other.

She moved with him so seamlessly it was as if she'd been born to be with him. And when the music ended, they danced on, oblivious, until laughter from the crowd woke them from the trance they were in. Cam smiled down at her, and Beth felt her heart take another tumble.

How could she love him so much? How could she risk her heart again? And how could she not?

"Hey, Cam!" They both looked to where Tony was standing at the edge of the dance floor. "If you're finished, I want you to meet someone."

"Go," Beth said, stepping out of his grasp and waving one hand. Grateful for the reprieve, she stepped off the dance floor. She could only take so much magic in one outing. She needed a little space to clear her head, or to hope for clarity, anyway. "I'll see you later."

"I'll hold you to that," Cam told her, lifting one hand to cup her cheek briefly.

That slight touch sent heat skittering through her,

and Beth knew she was in real trouble. She watched him stalk off to meet Tony, then she slipped into the crowd again. When a woman's hand took hold of her arm as she passed, Beth nearly groaned. She just wanted some time to herself. Maybe under the shade of a tree to help ease the heat crouching inside.

Her aunt Piper gave her a rueful smile. "I saw that performance. You guys still dance together like you were born to it."

Beth turned to look back at the dance floor, where other couples were moving in tandem to another song.

"Piper," she said, looking back to the other woman, "I don't know what I'm doing."

Her aunt winked. "Looked to me like you did."

"Dancing? Sure." Beth laughed a little and hated that it sounded so pitiful even to her own ears. "But everything else? It's a mystery to me."

Piper laid one arm around Beth's shoulders and steered her through the crowd until they found a semi-deserted spot. "Honey, you still love him, don't you?"

She could have denied it, but what would have been the point? "Ridiculous, isn't it?"

"No." Piper shook her head, her short, dark brown hair swinging into an arc and then settling back into its perfect cut. "It's not."

Beth wanted to believe her. Piper had always been more of an older sister to Beth than an aunt, and they'd shared a lot of secrets over the years. Piper knew all about Beth and Cam. Knew what had happened. Knew what it had done to Beth. How Cam's leaving had sent her into a sort of spiral that she'd had to dig her way out of on her own.

"Am I just supposed to get over it?" she asked, not really expecting an answer. "To move on and not remember what happened before?"

"Of course not," Piper said quickly. "How could you? It was horrible, and at the time I wanted to find Cam Guthrie myself and slap him silly for what he did."

Beth's lips curved at the thought and at the loving loyalty.

"But, honey, you already got past it." Piper tucked Beth's hair behind her ear. "You built a good life. You stand on your own two feet and don't owe anyone an explanation for what you do with that life."

"Thanks. I do know that. Really." Beth sighed and said, "It's just I don't know if I can let myself love him this time. What if he leaves again? What if we break up and I drop into that black hole I was in before?"

"And what if the world stops turning and we all fly into space?" Piper laughed, hugged Beth hard, then stood back and gripped her shoulders. "You don't get a guarantee, Beth. You get chances. Whether you take them or not is up to you."

"And I don't know if I should."

"I do." Piper waited for Beth's gaze to meet hers. "Go for it, sweetie. Always take the chance when you get it. Living a life with regrets isn't the way to go."

Beth heard something in her aunt's voice that worried her. "Hey. Are you okay?"

A bright smile lit Piper's face. "Of course. Aren't I always?" Her gaze slid past Beth then and she said, "Oh, damn."

Beth looked and her shoulders slumped. Her mom, Ava, was here, arm in arm with Keith Cooper. All of Beth's life, she'd known that "Uncle Keith" was in love with her mother. The weird thing was that Ava never seemed to notice. Since Beth's father died, Keith had been around Ava at all times. And it looked like that wasn't going to stop.

"I really thought after they got home from Europe that Keith would give up and move on," Beth muttered. "Does Mom have zero clue that the man is crazy about her?"

Piper said only, "Don't worry about your mother, Beth. Ava's a smart woman. She's not as oblivious as you think she is."

It didn't look like it to her. "I hope you're right."

In an instant, everything changed.

Suddenly the firefighters were hustling kids off the trucks, jumping into their uniforms and driving off, sirens screaming. Most in the crowd cupped their hands over their ears, and Beth winced at the noise. "What do you suppose is happening?"

She glanced at Piper, but before she could answer, Sebastian and Sutton rushed up to them.

"There's a fire at one of our WinJet plants," Sebastian said. "I just got a call from the security company."

"The plant outside Royal," Sutton put in to clarify, since there were a few manufacturing plants to take care of the private plane orders they received every year.

The twins were identical in every way, and right now even their grim expressions were mirrors of each other.

"At least it's Saturday," Piper said quickly. "So no one's there to get injured."

"No," Sutton muttered darkly. "We're pushing a deadline, so we're running two shifts. They're working today."

"Oh, my God..." Beth's whisper was lost in the nervous, excited chatter springing up all around them.

"We're headed over there now," Sebastian said, and grabbed Sutton's upper arm.

"I'll be right behind you. I'm getting my car," Piper informed them.

"What's going on?" Cam came up behind Beth, and she was grateful to feel his steady calm.

"There's a fire," she said. "At one of our manufacturing plants." Turning to look at him, she added, "I'm riding over with Piper, but first I have to find Gracie. Let her know I'm leaving."

Cam looked to Piper and said, "You go ahead. I'll bring Beth."

Piper looked at the two of them and nodded. "See you there. I have to find Ava."

"I'll tell Zeke. He can find Luke," Beth said as Piper hurried away.

"Come on." Cam grabbed her hand and led her through the crowd. In one corner of her mind, Beth was amazed at how the crowd seemed to part right in front of him. People made way. Whether it was Cam himself or the fact that they could tell there was an emergency, she didn't know. But she wouldn't have been surprised to find it was simply Cam's commanding personality that had people stepping out of his way.

She paused when she saw Zeke, still on the dance floor. This time, he was doing a complicated ten-step with his friend, Reagan Sinclair. Reagan's long, dark brown hair flew out behind her like a velvet cape as she laughed up into Zeke's face.

"Sorry to break this up," Beth said, tugging at Zeke's arm. "Reagan, I really need Zeke."

"No problem." Reagan looked concerned but didn't slow them down with questions.

Quickly Beth explained everything and watched the fun in Zeke's eyes drain away and be replaced by solemn resolve.

"Reagan, gotta go," he said. Then he turned to Beth. "I'll find Luke and we'll meet you at the plant."

Beth and Cam set off again and found Gracie near the donation table talking to James Harris. It only took a minute to explain what was happening and that she needed Gracie to take charge of the rest of the party.

Cam's truck was parked close by, and before long they were on the highway leading out of Royal. "So talk to me," he said. "This is a WinJet plant?"

"Yes," she replied, willing them to go faster. "Sebastian said there's a whole shift working there today to make up time on back orders. If the fire..."

She didn't even want to think about it, really. A fire sweeping through the plant could spread quickly. Anyone caught inside was in real danger. There were so many potentially flammable things stored there. Chemicals used in working on the planes, paints, fiberglass... Fire was the absolute worst thing that could happen. She could only pray that everyone had gotten out safely.

Cam didn't ask any more questions and didn't offer meaningless platitudes, for which she was grateful. He only grabbed her hand and held on. Beth curled her fingers around his, thankful for the support. As they neared the turnoff, she could see thick black smoke snaking up into the sky and twisting in the breeze. "Oh, God."

Cam took the turnoff and drove straight to the front of the parking lot, where Beth's family was already gathered, watching the firefighters attack the blaze. Beth was out of the car before he'd put it in Park, and Cam wasn't far behind her.

Beth grabbed Sutton's arm. "Did everyone get out?"

He looked down at her and his features were tight. "Everyone's out, but three of the men on the line were hurt."

"How bad?"

"Bad enough," Sebastian said darkly, and nodded a greeting as Cam came up behind Beth. "There's smoke inhalation, a couple of second-degree burns, and one of the guys broke his leg when he jumped off a ladder to get out."

"But they *are* out and they're going to be fine," Zeke put in.

Absently, Beth noted Cam draping one arm around her shoulder. She liked it. It spoke of solidarity and silent comfort, both of which she needed at the moment.

Sebastian turned to look at all of them, and his gaze flickered briefly when he noticed Cam's arm around Beth. But he stayed on subject when he said, "The men have already been transported to Royal hospital. They're being taken care of, and everyone else is being checked out by the EMTs, just in case. The real question is how did the fire start in the first place?"

Good point. Beth watched Nathan Battles, his face set in grim lines, walk up to join them. "Sorry to see this, but the fire captain says they'll have it out in another hour."

"Can we go in then?"

Nathan took off his hat and ran his forearm across his forehead. "Probably not. The fire marshal has to inspect the property, then the arson inspector will be out to do the same."

"Arson?" Beth repeated, shocked at the idea.

"You can't be serious," Piper said. "Nate, you know us."

"I'm not saying the fire was deliberately set," Nathan clarified a second later. "That's standard procedure for a fire. We have to find out how the blaze started."

"He's right," Sebastian said, never taking his gaze off the firefighters now shooting foam at the flames licking at the roof. "We take care of business. First priority is making sure our people are safe. The rest we'll handle as it comes."

Sutton moved off to talk to the fire captain, and a moment later, Sebastian, Luke and Zeke joined him. Piper and Ava stood to one side with Keith. The expressions on their faces told Beth they were feeling as stunned and worried as she was.

Looking up at Cam, she asked, "Can you drive me to the hospital? I want to check on the injured men."

"Sure," he said. He caught her hand and Beth threaded her fingers through his. His warm, steady grip on her hand made her feel complete in a way she hadn't in years. In spite of everything that had happened between them, she realized in a flash that Cam was still the only man she wanted. The only man she would ever love.

She just didn't know what that meant. For either of them.

Nine

Over the next week, the Wingates concentrated on the aftereffects of the fire. The family gathered at the main house for more meetings than Beth could count. Piper was staying with them rather than making the drive from Dallas every day, and Ava and Keith were practically inseparable. Beth wanted to worry about that, but frankly she already had too much going on in her mind.

Not the least of which was why she hadn't heard from Camden since the day of the fire. He had to know what she was going through. So why was he avoiding her? Was he regretting becoming involved with her again? Was he trying to subtly let her know that she couldn't depend on him? If so, he was doing a hell of a job.

And besides Camden and the fire concerns, Beth still had her foundations to take care of. She had a lot of things going on and she couldn't exactly say *Sorry, I'm mentally fried and have no time to garner your donations.* So, in between worrying about Cam and attending the family meetings, she was running around town trying to make sure she didn't let anyone down.

Which was why taking a break for lunch with Piper and Gracie felt like a vacation.

Especially at the Courtyard shops. Only four miles outside Royal, it felt like a different world. Oak trees shaded the area in front of the small coffee stand that sold cakes, cookies and espresso-based drinks both iced and hot. There were a dozen delicate round tables that boasted bright pink umbrellas and iron scrollwork chairs. The café was kept busy by all of the shoppers thronging to the eclectic gathering of stores at the Courtyard.

The property used to be a ranch and the big red barn was still standing. Now, though, it housed Priceless, an antiques store and crafting studio. There were shops for local craftsmen making everything from artisanal soaps to stained glass, and every Saturday, booths sprang up like mushrooms for a farmers market. All in all, the place almost demanded that you relax. Sit for a while. Do some retail therapy and take a mental break. Just what Beth needed.

"There was a report on the radio this morning. The men who were injured are saying the sprinkler system at the plant malfunctioned." Gracie winced as she said it, obviously not wanting to heap more trouble on the situation.

And there went the break.

"I know," Beth said, and glanced at Piper before turning back to Gracie. She and the family had agreed to keep what they'd found between them, but Beth considered Gracie family. They'd been friends forever, they worked closely together, and Gracie had proved herself time and again to be extremely trustworthy.

So Beth didn't feel the slightest twinge of guilt telling her old friend exactly what was happening. "The injured men have all hired lawyers. They contacted us yesterday."

"Lawyers?" Gracie repeated, looking from one to the other of the women. "That doesn't sound good."

"No, it isn't." Piper picked up her coffee and took a sip. "They're talking about suing the company. Their lawyers made us aware that a formal suit will be filed within the month." She set her cup down and leaned back in her chair. "It's not exactly unexpected, but it is one more thing landing on top of an already miserable situation."

"Sebastian's furious," Beth said. "Not with the

employees so much as he is with the whole mess. He's determined to get to the bottom of how this happened in the first place. It doesn't help that we still haven't been allowed back into the plant."

Leaning forward, she kept her voice down so no one else would overhear. "He and Sutton have done an internal investigation already. They've been checking over safety inspection reports, and, apparently, the company wasn't up-to-date on the inspections."

"You're kidding," Gracie murmured. "That doesn't sound right."

"No, it doesn't." Piper frowned thoughtfully. "We've never had safety issues at any of our companies, so there's obviously something wrong. We just don't know what it is."

Gracie took a breath and blew it out. "What does this mean for you guys?"

"It means," Piper said quietly, "there's going to be a big payoff to the injured men, obviously. Beyond that, no one knows yet."

"The company's healthy," Beth added, "so no one's worried about having to pay out a settlement. The real problem is finding out that someone in the company's been cutting corners with safety. We can't survive that. No company could."

That fact had made for some very uncomfortable conversations at the house this last week. Trying to wrap their heads around the idea that someone within the company, someone they knew and trusted, had sabotaged them. Though it was a horrible thought, it was the only thing that made sense.

It had to be an insider who was behind the safety inspections, the malfunctioning sprinklers and maybe even the fire itself. But who? And why?

“So what’s next?” Gracie kept her voice low and glanced at the table beside them as an older couple got up to leave. When they were gone, she added, “Is there a plan for handling all of this?”

“Not much of one yet,” Piper admitted. “Between Sebastian, Sutton, Luke and Zeke, there are too many ideas and not one they’ve settled on yet.”

“It’s not just the guys, either,” Beth said. “Mom’s putting her two cents in and driving Sebastian a little nuts with it. And Piper and I spend most of our time telling them all to calm down.” Which was funny, considering what she herself had said to Justin not too long ago. *Telling someone to calm down never makes them calm down.*

“And we’re bringing Miles into this.” Beth’s younger brother, Miles Wingate, had his own company, Steel Security, based out of Chicago. It was already one of the most acclaimed security companies in the world, and since Miles was family, he would know better than anyone how important it was to solve the mystery of the fire and the safety inspections.

“That’s a really good idea.”

Piper nodded at Gracie. "Sebastian's idea."

"Well," Gracie acknowledged, "he's brilliant, so I'm not surprised."

"Don't ever tell Baz he's brilliant, it'll go to his head." Beth picked up her iced tea and took a sip. She watched Gracie stand, get the newspaper the older couple had left on their table and then sit down again. "Oh, please don't show me any Wingates Are Evil headlines."

Gracie laughed and shook her head. "Promise. I'm just checking my lottery numbers."

"Well, if ever there was a day for some good news," Beth said, "today is it. So win enough to pay for lunch, okay?"

"I'll try." Gracie opened the paper and pulled her ticket from her black leather bag.

Beth was watching her compare her ticket to the numbers in the paper, and she actually saw Gracie go pale. "What is it?" she demanded, reaching for her friend's arm. "Gracie, what happened?"

Gracie lifted her gaze to Beth's and opened and closed her mouth for a couple of seconds, but no sound escaped. Finally she took a deep, shuddering breath and managed to say, "I…uh. Here." She handed over the paper and her ticket. Swallowing hard, she said, "You look. Double-check me."

"Double-check?" Beth repeated. "You either won something or you didn't."

But she dutifully compared the numbers on

Gracie's ticket to the winning combination in the paper. Then she checked it again. And a third time. Excitement exploded inside her. Stunned, she stared at Gracie.

"What is it?" Piper's voice broke into the taut silence. "Will somebody please tell me what's going on?"

Beth laughed, shocked and happy and starting to really worry about Gracie. "Oh, I can tell you, but you might not believe me." Laughter rang in her voice as she said, "Gracie's buying lunch. She just won sixty million dollars."

"What?" Piper grabbed the ticket and the paper.

Delighted, Beth, still laughing, grabbed her best friend's hand and squeezed.

Gracie doubled over and said, "I think I'm going to be sick."

Cam thought it was for the best that he and Beth hadn't seen each other in a week. It forced them both to evaluate what was happening between them and decide where to go with it. The day of the fire she'd been shocked and worried, and she'd needed him. But since then, he hadn't heard from her, and Cam figured there was a reason for that.

Bottom line, no matter what he felt when he was around her, he wasn't going to set himself up for another princess betrayal.

Beth was still royalty here in Royal, Texas. And in

spite of his wealth, Camden was still a half–Native American cowboy. Things hadn't changed, not really. Society in Royal would always be two separate tiers, and climbing that particular ladder never went well—not that he was interested in their damn ladder anyway.

New money would never be looked at with the same reverence and respect as old money, and he didn't care to try to change things. Actually he didn't give a shit what anyone thought of him. He was exactly who he had always been. He just had more cash on hand now. And rich was definitely better than poor, he could admit.

But building his own life here—on his own—made more sense than revisiting the past with Beth and trying to remodel it. Loving her and yes, he had to admit that he loved her even more now than he once had, didn't change anything. Hard to acknowledge, but dangerous to ignore.

"What are you thinking about that's putting that scowl on your face?"

He looked at Tony and scowled deeper. "I'm not scowling."

"Right." Tony chuckled. He picked up the drawings of his ideas for the baseball camp that he'd spread out on Cam's dining room table and said, "It's Beth."

"It's none of your business."

"Sure." He chuckled again. "I saw you two dancing at the party last week. Just like old times."

If he scowled any harder, Cam was pretty sure his face would just crack. "Beth isn't on my mind." Lies.

"Sure she's not. So you're just nervous about the TCC meeting?"

"I'm not nervous," Cam argued, and this time he meant it. Did he want to be a member of the TCC? Yes. If he didn't get in, would it be the end of his plans for the future? Hell, no. "Am I twelve? I'll get in or I won't. Period."

It wasn't nerves. It was…concern. That was different, he assured himself. The vote on new members was tomorrow night, and Cam would be there. Maybe he shouldn't, but damned if he'd hide and let all the other members know that he was worried how the vote would go.

Tony would be there, too, since he was already a member. Big-league baseball catcher, local businessman, of course he was in. Now it was Cam's turn, and he'd find out soon if Burt Wheeler had poisoned the well against him. Sure, he'd put Cam's name up for a vote, but he'd also had a week to talk to his friends and convince them to vote no. Hell, a part of Cam couldn't even blame Burt for it.

He'd lost his daughter and needed someone to blame. Cam was the lucky winner.

And all of this thinking wasn't doing a damn sight of good, either.

"You ready to go?" Cam's new lawyer was expecting them to come by and sign the paperwork to get Tony's camp up and running.

"Sure." Tony rolled up the drawings he'd had made and slipped a rubber band around them. "I'll take my own car, though. I've got a date after the meeting with the lawyers."

"Fine." Cam didn't have a damn date. He'd be coming back to his house. Alone. Just like he'd been all week. Hell. He couldn't even get a good night's sleep anymore because his bedroom held the ghost of Beth. Her scent. Her laugh. Her touch. Wouldn't it just figure that the only woman he wanted was the woman he was steering clear of. Coming home to Texas had been a dance of misery and joy, and he wasn't sure from day to day which one would take precedence.

Changing the subject abruptly, he said, "Those are good drawings for your camp."

Tony grinned. "It's going to be great. Still can't thank you enough for the land."

"You don't have to. It's going to be good for both of us." He smiled just thinking about it, and that was a good thing.

"You're still pitching, I'm still catching," Tony said with a shrug. "We still make a good team."

And that was a bit of the joy in coming back to Royal. Reconnecting with old friends. Charting a future that held exactly what he wanted. And if he didn't get *everything* he wanted? Well, he'd just have to deal with it.

Beth took Gracie to her mother's house and left her in good hands. The whole Diaz family was in tears—well, except for Gracie's little brother, who immediately went online to shop.

The shock of winning the lottery really hadn't worn off for Gracie yet. And when it did, the reality of it would put her into another wild emotional spin. Beth was thrilled for her. Suddenly all those dreams Gracie had built in her mind over the years were going to come true.

Of course, her life was going to become crazy once news of her win became public. She'd be hounded for interviews and have people she'd never known coming to her looking for a handout.

"And I might need a new assistant," Beth muttered. After all, why would Gracie keep a job she no longer needed? "Oh, that's a horrible thought. Who's going to help me keep all of this straight? Oh, Gracie… I already miss you."

When her phone rang, Beth saw her sister's name pop up on the screen and smiled. Harley had been gone from Texas for years and Beth really missed her. Right now, though, she was jealous of her little sister because Harley, living in Thailand, was well out of the controversy over WinJet.

"Hey, Harley!"

"Hey, yourself." Her sister's voice came across the Bluetooth perfectly. Beth didn't know why Sutton complained about the connection from Beth's car.

She stopped at a red light and said, "How are you and my adorable nephew?"

"We're both good," Harley said. She added wryly, "Probably better than all of you guys are. How's the investigation going?"

"Slowly," Beth admitted. They'd had a conference call with Harley and Miles the night of the fire so all of the siblings were on the same page. "It's only been a week, but Sebastian and Sutton are like twin pit bulls with bones. They're hovering over every report, talking to the experts, huddling with Nathan Battles and the fire chief at every opportunity..."

"Sounds bad."

The light changed and Beth stepped on the gas, heading down Main Street and keeping an eagle eye out for people backing out of parking spots. "It is bad, Harley. Being at the house these days is just a nightmare. I'm actually jealous of Luke and Zeke living in the guesthouse. At least they get to escape it once in a while.

"And it doesn't look like it's going to get better. Sebastian's calling Miles in to investigate."

"Well, if there's anything there, Miles will find it."

"True." And that worried her, too. What would Miles find? Was WinJet guilty of sloppy safety procedures? It was hard to believe, but right now that's what it was looking like. Unless their mysterious insider had somehow changed things so it appeared that the Wingate family wasn't concerned about safety.

So who exactly was behind that? They had to know, even if the answer would be more painful than the question.

"How's Mom?"

"She's…" Beth paused to find the right word. Ava had been right in the thick of all of this since the moment it started. For a woman who really hadn't spent much time with the family business, their mother was like a force of nature. "Tougher than I thought. She's in the middle of it all, and Uncle Keith is volunteering his time to help Mom and the twins find the truth."

"He's still panting after Mom?"

"Thank you." Beth shook her head, made a right turn at the next block and pulled into the first parking spot she found. She couldn't concentrate on driving while she was dealing with all of this, too. "I thought I was the only one who was convinced Keith was desperately in love with her."

"You're not. The last time I was in Royal, it seemed so obvious to me. Even when Dad was alive, Keith was smitten."

"Smitten?" Beth smiled to herself.

"It's a perfectly good word. And I wonder why Mom doesn't see it."

"Piper says she does and we shouldn't worry about it."

"I guess Piper would know," Harley mused, but didn't sound confident. Then she half covered the phone and said, "Daniel, we'll go for a walk as soon as I'm finished talking to Aunt Beth, okay?"

"Give him my love." Beth sighed. "I really miss you guys. Daniel's going to be six feet tall the next time I see him."

"He's only four," Harley replied, laughing. "And you could come to Thailand for a visit."

"Trust me," Beth said on a sigh, "I wish I was there right now."

"I bet." Harley paused. "Look, Beth, I'm actually calling for a more personal reason."

"Everything okay?" Sister alarm bells went off in her mind and Beth sat up straighter.

"Yes, sure. I told you, we're fine. The problem is Zest," she admitted.

"Your nonprofit?" Beth waved at Marva Wilson, walking her ancient beagle down the sidewalk. "What's wrong?"

"We're not making enough money to stay alive," Harley confessed. "I've been dipping into my trust to make ends meet because I can't bear the thought of letting down the women who depend on me. And, frankly, I could really use your fund-raising skills."

Worry rippled through Beth. She hated to think of her little sister losing the foundation that meant so much to her. She also dreaded the thought of Harley dipping into a trust fund meant to take care of her and her son.

Harley had helped countless women to stand on their own two feet. To help them make enough money to support their families. To build better lives. Naturally Beth's little sister wouldn't give up finding ways to keep that kind of commitment going.

"Of course I'll help."

Harley sighed in relief. "Thank you. I knew I could count on you. Honestly, Beth, you have no idea how much this means to me."

"Yeah, I do." Her sister had the biggest heart of them all, and Beth would do whatever she could to make sure that heart didn't get broken. "And you can absolutely count on me to help any way I can." Her mind was already spinning with ideas on how to pull this off.

Before she lost Gracie as her assistant, Beth was going to drag her into helping work this out. "I'm sitting in a parking space off Main Street right now, so I can't really get into anything specific."

"Ohh. I miss Main Street. Where are you parked?"

Beth looked up. "I'm across the street from the ice-cream parlor."

Harley sighed. "That's so mean to tell me that."

"Sorry," Beth said on a laugh. "I meant I'm by the tire store."

"A lie, but easier to take. Thanks."

Beth laughed again. "Let me come up with some ideas, and I'll call you next week and we can decide which way to go."

"I already feel better, Beth. You are the best sister ever."

"Also your only sister..."

"Quality over quantity," Harley said, and made Beth laugh.

"Go take my nephew for a walk and don't worry. We'll fix this."

"Thanks again. Talk to you next week."

Beth fired up her car, backed out of her space and lifted one hand in a wave to whoever it was who honked at her in protest. Back on the road toward home, Beth thought about Harley's problem, already working out ideas on how to help.

She was beyond grateful for the task. Not only could she help her sister, but this gave her something else to think about besides the WinJet situation. Her entire family was on task with that anyway.

And though she had plenty of foundations to watch over and worry about, Harley's was personal and enough of a distraction to keep her thoughts from straying to Cam.

A week since she'd seen him. Talked to him. Touched him. She'd lived fifteen years without him, and now it felt as if she couldn't draw a breath without missing him.

The day of the fire, Cam had been…essential. From the start, he'd held her hand, comforted her and offered support. He hadn't tried to take over or tell her what to do or how to feel, but he *had* been a rock when it most mattered to her.

"But since then…" She shook her windblown hair out of her eyes and gritted her teeth. Since that horrible day, she hadn't seen or heard from Camden Guthrie.

Not a word. Not even a phone call. He'd disappeared, much as he had fifteen years ago. For one day, he'd been there for her and then…poof. Gone. Did he think that the crisis had disappeared? Was he deliberately staying away to let her know that she couldn't count on him? That nothing had really changed between them? Or was this the universe telling her to forget about him and move on? That nothing between them was ever going to last?

She didn't know anymore.

Sebastian was on the phone when Beth got home. She heard him all the way down the hall from their father's study. He was furious, and though he wasn't shouting, he was talking so loud the otherwise quiet house echoed with his voice.

Wondering what new crisis had struck while she was out, Beth hurried down the hall, her heels tapping against the red tiled floor. She didn't pass anyone else in the house and when she turned into the study, she knew why. Everyone was gathered there, watching Sebastian as if they were the audience studying an actor's every move.

Ava and Piper had the two guest chairs, and the guys were all standing in a semicircle behind them. The study was both familiar and foreign. When Beth's father was alive, no one had been allowed in. He had liked his "alone" time and ran the many Wingate businesses from this well-appointed massive room.

There were floor-to-ceiling bookcases on three of the walls and an elegantly tiled fireplace, big enough for a tall man to stand up in, on the fourth. The walls were dotted with framed photos of Trent Wingate alongside presidents and moguls, and two of Piper's oil paintings of the house and grounds.

Sebastian and Sutton shared this space now, though it had always seemed to Beth that Sebastian was the most comfortable in it. At the moment, Sebastian was practically growling into the phone as he paced furiously from one side of the room to the other.

Beth sidled up to Zeke. "What's going on?"

"We got a report that the arson inspector can't rule out the possibility that the fire might have been deliberately set."

"What?" Shock had made her voice a lot louder than she'd planned.

Sebastian fired a hard look at her, silently telling her to be quiet. She waved one hand at him, unmoved by his impatience, then moved close to Piper and leaned down. "Is Zeke serious? There was an arsonist?"

Piper shrugged and said, "No one's sure yet. Apparently, the inspector said it was 'unclear.' They're going to continue the investigation."

Sebastian shot her a glowering look now as he paced back and forth behind his desk.

Piper made a face at him and kept talking, though she did lower her voice a little in deference to Sebastian's blood pressure. "And that means we can't get into the building yet. That's driving Baz crazy of course, and Sutton's right behind him."

"It's making us all a little crazy," Beth said. "Is Miles coming out soon?"

"No word on that yet," Piper told her. "Apparently he's got plenty going on right now and can't get away."

"Hey, he's a Wingate, too." A little pissy, Beth said, "Why does Miles get to choose to stay out of this?"

"Believe me when I tell you Sebastian is with you on that."

"I bet." Beth sighed and dropped to one knee

while she watched Sebastian arguing with whichever poor soul was on the other end of the phone.

"How's Gracie doing?" Piper asked.

"I think she's in shock." Beth smiled. "When I dropped her off, her mother was making margaritas to celebrate and her little brother was looking up Porsches online."

"That's fantastic!" Piper laughed. "I'm so glad for her. But this is going to be hard on her, too."

"Oh, I know." Beth was still worried about her friend and the bundle of cash that had dropped into her lap. "I don't think she's figured that part out yet. She's going to be a big celebrity when word gets out and Gracie's not going to like that."

"She's got friends—like you. That's going to help."

"I hope so."

Sebastian hung up and the sudden silence in the room was deafening. His features were tight and grim, and there was a dark gleam in his green eyes. He looked at the family, set both hands on his hips and said, "You heard most of that. The investigation's ongoing. They're not saying it was arson, but they're not saying it wasn't, either."

He rubbed one hand through his hair. "If it was arson, that could make the insurance coverage problematic unless we can prove who did it and that we didn't have a hand in it."

"No one would think we would burn down our own plant," Luke argued.

"No sane person," Sebastian agreed. "But it would put us in the bizarre position of having to prove we *didn't* do it. Hard to prove a negative."

"What happened to innocent until proven guilty?" Zeke wondered aloud.

"Good question," Sebastian snapped.

"What does Nathan say?" Ava spoke up suddenly. Not surprisingly, Keith was standing behind her.

"Nate can't do anything about this," Sebastian said. "This is all the fire marshal and the arson inspector."

"Which means we're screwed…for now," Sutton put in. "Is Miles coming out?"

Sebastian frowned. "He's busy, he said. But I'll get him out here."

"I can do that," Ava offered.

Beth thought that was probably the best way to go. No way could Miles stand against their mother.

Sebastian nodded at her. "Good, Mom. That might work. If it doesn't, I'll call him again." His gaze swept the people in the room, one by one. "Anyone have something to add?"

"Well…" Everyone turned to look at Zeke. He smiled, swiped one hand across his jaw and shrugged. "I do have something. Not about the fire, though."

"Good," Sutton said. "I can use other news."

"This qualifies then." Zeke looked over at his twin, then announced, "I'm engaged to Reagan Sinclair."

Ten

Zeke was *engaged*?

"Since when?" Beth had just seen them dancing together at the fund-raiser. She knew the two of them had been good friends for a long time, but this was the first she'd heard about a romance.

"Since today," Zeke said, and held up one hand when the questions started flying from every corner of the room. "It's sort of an engagement of convenience," he explained with another casual shrug. "To claim her inheritance from her grandmother, Reagan has to be married. So…we're hoping the engagement announcement will do the trick for the lawyers."

"Seriously? A fake engagement?" Luke shook his head at his twin.

"Hey, we're the only ones who will know it's a fake," Zeke said. "To everyone else, it's the real deal. I even bought her a ring."

"Uh-huh," Sutton interrupted. "And if being engaged isn't enough to fulfill the demands of the will?"

Zeke grinned. "Then we'll get married."

"You're crazy," his twin muttered, loud enough for everyone to hear.

"We're twins," he pointed out. "So if I am, you are, too. Anyway, Reagan's a good friend, and I want to help her out. If she can't get the inheritance without a wedding, we're going to have one."

Okay. Beth stood up. There had just been way too many big announcements in the last week or so. The fire. The lawsuit. Gracie. Zeke. *And don't forget Cam*, her mind whispered.

If only she could.

While the family talked about Zeke's engagement and the fire inspector, Beth slipped out of the study. She'd had more than enough for the day, and all she really wanted now was a hot bath and bed.

But she wasn't going to get it right away.

"Beth…"

She stopped at the foot of the sweeping staircase leading to the second floor. With one hand on the glossy walnut banister, Beth turned to watch Piper approach.

"What's going on with you and Cam?"

"Nothing." Short conversation, but what else could she say? As far as she knew, there was nothing *real* between her and Cam. Beth loved him, she could acknowledge that to herself. But given the fact that she hadn't heard from him in a week, she suspected that his feelings for her stopped at the bedroom.

"Come on, sweetie." Piper tipped her head to one side. "We both know that's not true."

"Fine. Do I love him? Yes," Beth admitted. "Does that change anything? No."

"Oh, Beth," Piper said, sighing. "It changes everything."

"Not always." She had thought that they were finding their way back to each other, but in the last week Beth had realized she was wrong. A relationship couldn't survive if only one of the people involved was in love.

"He hasn't even called me, Piper." Her fingers tightened on the balustrade. "In a week. Nothing. And he knows what's going on with us right now. With me. If he gave a flying damn, wouldn't he have come by or phoned, just to check in? See how I'm doing? Say hello?"

"You're right," Piper said. "He does know what's going on. But he could think that calling would be intruding on a family situation."

"No." Beth laughed at the idea and shook her head. "Cam's never had trouble 'intruding' if he was going after something he wanted."

"Fine. Then maybe he's waiting for you to call him."

Surprised, Beth looked at her aunt. "You think I should be calling Cam? I should be the one to go to him?"

"Would it kill you?"

"It might," Beth argued. "He's the one who left me, remember?"

"Of course I do. I also remember that it was fifteen years ago."

"Oh, is there a time limit on betrayal that I wasn't aware of?" Beth's eyes went wide with faux shock. "Someone should have told me."

"That's not what I meant and I think you know it."

"Okay, do you remember how well I handled it when Cam left?" Beth hated the memory of how losing him had practically destroyed her. Hated even thinking about it.

With her heart shattered, Beth had gone off to college and become someone she didn't even know. She drank too much. Slept around. Drove too fast, laughed too loud and damn near flunked out of college. And then her father had arrived out of the blue. She'd fought him of course because she hadn't wanted advice. Hadn't wanted to think of anything but the next adventure she could use to bury her pain.

But Trent Wingate wasn't a man you could easily ignore. He'd given her one of his famous *sit down, shut up and listen* talks and, thankfully, it had gotten through to her. Especially the part where he'd told her that he was disappointed in her, letting a man dictate how she acted.

He was right. And oh, how she'd hated to admit it. Because of what Cam had done, she'd completely lost herself. That was the day she had realized that her future was up to her to design. She'd turned it all around, graduated at the top of her class with a business degree and had come home to Royal to join Wingate Enterprises.

"I let my own life go to hell because Cam left me," she admitted, though it cost her a ding to her pride. "It was pitiful, Piper. I needed him so much that without him, I was completely lost. I never want to be that way again."

Piper grabbed her hand and held on. "I know how hard it was, sweetie. But do you really think you could ever let that happen to you again?"

"Not a chance." She wasn't that naive young girl pinning all of her dreams on the boy she loved. Now she stood on her own. She was strong enough to sway with the wind, not break. Beth had learned that she could make it on her own and that sharing her life with someone was a choice—not a necessity. She'd never really thought about it before, but without the pain of losing Cam, would she have discovered who she really was?

"Then what's the problem?" Piper shook her head. "Beth, everyone wants to be needed. Even the strongest man needs to be loved as much as anyone else. And so do you. You're right. You did fall apart when Cam left. But you also pulled yourself back together.

"You're the one who made the choices for your life. You built a career you can be proud of. You became a terrific woman with friends and family who love you. All of *that* happened because Cam left, too."

That was probably all true, she thought, knowing that if Cam had stayed, she would have made different choices because she'd have had different opportunities. Would that life have been better? She'd never know.

What she did know was that she liked who she was. Liked her life.

"Beth, what if Cam's waiting to see if you need him?"

She hadn't considered that, but she wasn't convinced. If he was waiting for her to call him, why hadn't he told her that? And that thought didn't even make sense to her.

Rubbing the spot between her eyebrows in a futile attempt to ease a budding headache, Beth heard Piper say, "If you don't make a move, you'll never know what you could have had. Are you willing to live with that kind of regret?"

She looked at her aunt. "Shouldn't you be telling Cam the same thing? Shouldn't he be the one to come to me?"

"Is this about winning?" Piper asked. "Or about love?"

"Maybe it's both."

"No, it can't be. If you're both trying to win, then you both lose."

Beth frowned at her aunt because she just might have a point. But wasn't it supposed to be the guy who did the chasing? The groveling, if necessary?

"Mmm-hmm." Looking completely pleased with herself, Piper added, "I'm glad you're willing to think about it, anyway. All I'm saying is, if you want something badly enough, you find a way to make it work."

Really hard to argue with something that made sense, and Beth was just too tired to try.

"Okay, that's enough of the well-meant lecture portion of our evening." Beth turned and headed up the stairs. "I want a bath."

"A bath is a good time to do some serious thinking…" Piper called after her.

Beth should have brought a bottle of wine with her.

The following night, the Texas Cattleman's Club was crowded with members coming in for the monthly meeting. The outside of the place hadn't changed too much while Cam had been gone. The building had been there forever, a piece of Royal history.

The TCC was a large, rambling single-story building made of dark stone and weathered wood, and boasted a steep slate roof. Once women had been welcomed into the club, the interior had undergone some major changes, according to Tony. The walls were painted a cream color that softened all the heavy dark beams lining the walls and the high ceilings.

Polished dark wood floors carried the marks of generations, with more than a few scars made by indiscriminate spur-wearing by the members. Hunting trophies and historical photos and artifacts hung on the walls, and heavy brown leather furniture invited people to sit and talk for a while.

Here in one of the big meeting rooms, though, banquet style, straight-backed chairs were set out for the members attending the meeting. Cam decided to stand against the wall and Tony was right beside him.

"How's Beth?" Tony asked.

"No idea," Cam answered through gritted teeth. She hadn't called him once all week. She'd been glad enough to have him with her the day of the fire. But since that day, nothing. It was as if she was deliberately shutting him out because she'd been vulnerable the last time they were together.

"Why the hell not?" Tony asked.

Cam looked at his old friend. "She hasn't called."

Tonight was the vote on new members and Cam had wanted to be there. Maybe a stupid decision, but if he was voted out he didn't want someone having to make a sympathetic phone call to let him know. Besides, he wanted to see who supported him and who didn't. Might be a masochistic move, but he'd always believed that *knowing* was better than *guessing*.

Sliding his gaze across the room, he spotted Burt Wheeler in a black blazer thrown on over his jeans and a blue-and-white-striped shirt. His cowboy hat was balanced on his upraised knee, and the frown on his face told Cam exactly how Burt was feeling about the upcoming vote.

"And you haven't bothered to call her," Tony said, "even though you know what crap she and her family are going through right now."

Yeah, he did know. Everyone in Royal was talking about the Wingates. There were stories online, reporters streaming in and out of town and theories about the fire—lots of theories. Some made sense, and others were as outlandish as saying space aliens started the blaze.

Through it all, Beth had not once reached out to him. Clearly she believed she didn't need him around, so Cam had kept his distance. But he was about done with that. Tomorrow, he and Beth were going to talk. Whether she liked it or not. He'd find a way to convince her that he was here now and he wasn't going anywhere. "No, I didn't. Because if she wanted me there, she'd have told me."

"How the hell did you two ever get together in the

first place?" Tony asked, astonished. "Two harder heads I've never seen."

"Thanks for the support, pal." He looked away and watched James Harris move slowly to the front of the room, stopping to shake hands and chat along the route. He envied James's easy, comfortable manner. The man was where he belonged and he knew it. Cam was still feeling like an imposter. The son of a couple of horse trainers becoming a member of the TCC? How his father would have laughed at the notion.

The rumble of conversation rose and fell like the tides, and, as an outsider, Cam could see friendships and wary enemies greeting each other.

"You're going to get in," Tony said easily.

"We'll find out soon." In his black suit, white shirt and black hat, Camden glanced around the room and felt as if he were wearing the uniform of the TCC. Every man there was dressed pretty much as he was. Good omen?

Then he spotted Justin McCoy, and everything in him coiled into a tight knot. The man walked through the room like he owned the place, which was just another irritation added to the rest. He carried his hat in his hand, and in the overhead light the man's receding blond hair looked almost white.

Cam stiffened as he followed Justin's progress through the room. He had to wonder if McCoy would still be welcome in the prestigious club if the members knew the truth about him.

Tony followed his gaze and sneered. "The only reason Justin's a member is because his great-great-whatever-grandfather was a founding member."

"Doesn't say much for the membership committee." Just looking at the man made Cam's hands curl into fists.

"No, really doesn't," Tony agreed.

When Justin spotted Cam, he headed right for him, a self-satisfied smirk on his face. It took everything he had for Cam to stay rooted to the spot. All he really wanted to do was meet him halfway and plant his fist in the other man's face.

Justin stopped right in front of him and gave Tony a brief nod of acknowledgment.

"You're not going to get in, you know."

Cam chuckled and his gaze never left Justin's. "You're the one reason that might be okay with me."

Justin flushed, and on his pale face, the red splotches were unmistakable.

"But me being a member isn't up to you, Justin. You just think you're important."

"You're not getting into this club," Justin repeated, then leaned in closer. "And you're not getting Beth. You don't deserve her."

A part of him might have always secretly believed that, but damned if he'd let Justin say it. "You don't want a war with me, Justin..."

"Guys, dial it down, okay?"

Cam ignored Tony's warning. "Because I'm going to tell you right now, I've got plenty of ammo to use against you if that's the way you want to go."

Justin flinched. Cam saw it in his eyes, but he still used bravado to talk his way out. "I'm not worried. Do what you want. Who here would ever believe Camden Guthrie against a McCoy?"

When Justin moved on, Tony leaned in and said. "Don't get yourself in a twist. The man's a dick. No one likes him. No one listens to him."

Justin McCoy was all that and more, Cam thought. He forced himself to put McCoy out of his mind and concentrate instead on his own future.

Beth saw it all.

Her gaze had fixed on Cam the moment she slipped into the meeting room. As if there was no one else in the place, she could see only him. He wore an elegantly cut suit and tie and held his black hat in his right hand. He and Tony were talking together when Justin came up and said something that had Cam's features turning to stone.

The confrontation didn't last long, and Beth really wanted to know what they'd been talking about. But a moment later, James Harris was calling the meeting to order.

Beth slunk down in her chair at the back of the room. She was there for the membership vote because she could at least cast her vote for Cam. But she didn't want him to see her until she was ready.

The Wingates had been members of the TCC for decades though it was only recently that women had been accepted. Even now though, there were still several of the old guard at the club who resented any female strolling through the hallowed halls of the Texas Cattleman's Club.

But, as more than one woman had said, *Too bad for them.*

Beth smiled at a couple of friends, then turned her attention to James. No matter how many times someone spoke up to interrupt him, he calmly kept the meeting on track. She didn't envy him the task of trying to ride herd on such a big group.

Quietly she watched the wealthiest, most influential people in Royal calling across the room like high school kids, laughing and talking. Her brothers were all here, too, and she thought of them all as creating a Wingate Wall against suspicion and gossip.

Everyone in town had had something to say about the fire at WinJet. They were all waiting to see what would happen next, and Beth was right there with them.

But tonight she wasn't thinking about the family or the company. Her thoughts were focused on Camden and what her aunt Piper had said to her the day before. *If they were both trying to win, they were both going to lose.*

When the vote was finally called, Beth raised her hand to vote yes on Cam's membership, and she was glad to see that her brothers did, too. And except for a small handful of Burt Wheeler's cronies—and Justin McCoy of course—the vote was overwhelmingly on Cam's side.

She looked at him in time to see him grin at Tony, and her heart did a quick leap. Cam was the one she wanted, and she'd realized earlier that day that Piper had a point. Why should she wait for him to come to her? Didn't she have the same right as a man to go after what she wanted ?

She smiled to herself at the realization. But tonight wasn't the time for her to face Camden and tell him how she felt. He was surrounded by people shaking his hand and welcoming him into the TCC. This was a night for him to concentrate on his win. She could wait until tomorrow.

Still smiling, she slipped out of her seat and headed for the door. She felt better than she had in more than a week. She'd made a decision to go for it. To risk it all for a chance at love and happiness. She whispered, "And I won't take no for an answer."

"Beth!"

She groaned and half-heartedly turned to wait for Justin McCoy. If Cam looked over here, he'd see her. Hopefully, he had as little interest in Justin as she did.

"I didn't know you were coming tonight," he said,

face flushed from rushing through the crowd to catch up with her.

She smiled up at him. "Well, my brothers and I wanted to be here to vote for Cam."

His lips thinned into such a fine line his mouth looked like a wrinkle in his chin. "I wish you hadn't done that."

"Well, I'm sorry you feel that way." Beth inched toward the door. "I really can't stay, Justin."

"Now, no need to rush off." He draped one arm around her shoulders and Beth squirmed out from under him.

"Justin…"

"Beth," he said patiently, "it's time you got past this infatuation with Camden Guthrie and realized that you and I are meant to be."

She blinked at him. Really, she couldn't even think of anything to say to that. How did you argue with someone who was so removed from reality?

"I understand you have some memories of Guthrie, but those are long dead. The future is for *us*."

"Justin, that's never going to happen."

He held on to her again, pulling her to his side, and Beth had to work harder this time to get him off her. She didn't want to make a scene—people were talking about the Wingates already. But if he didn't stop pawing at her, Beth might show him a few of the anti-male moves her brothers had taught her when she was a teenager.

Staring up into his eyes, she willed him to pay attention. "Listen to me, Justin. The answer to you is no. It will always be no."

"You heard the lady."

Beth jolted. She had been so focused on getting rid of Justin that she hadn't noticed the man she loved walking up to them. Now he and Tony were standing side by side, and Cam's gaze was fixed on Justin. No one else had really noticed anything going on because the noise level was loud enough to drown out anything.

All Beth could see was Cam. His dark eyes flashed with heat and banked fury, and she wished Justin McCoy to the other side of the planet. She laid one hand on his forearm and felt the tension in his body. "It's okay, Cam. I'm fine. And Justin's leaving."

"Yeah, he is," Cam said, staring at Justin with an angry glare before flicking a glance at Beth. "There's a lot of things I'm willing to take, but this isn't one of them."

"What're you talking about?" Beth moved closer to Cam.

He looked down at her again. "If you don't want me, that's fine. Your choice. But damned if I'll watch you hook up with this son of a bitch."

"Who're you calling an SOB?" Justin demanded.

"Excuse me?" Beth said, outraged that he would think she'd be interested in Justin. If he'd seen the man drape his arm around her, hadn't he also seen her trying to escape? "You just heard me tell him 'no' again."

"You're not saying it loud enough," Cam argued.

"The only way I could be louder is with a microphone."

"Stay out of this, Beth," Justin said.

"Agreed," Cam said, his gaze boring into Justin's. "This is between me and you." Cam kept his voice low enough that only their tight circle could hear him. "You think I'll let you anywhere near Beth when we both know damn well what you did to Julie."

"You don't know what you're talking about."

"What did he do?" Beth asked, shooting a wary look at Justin before turning her gaze back to Cam.

Cam speared Justin with a hot glare that should have set fire to what was left of his hair.

Speaking quietly to Beth, he said, "I promised Julie I'd never say a word about this. But she's gone now and damned if I'm going to let him strut around here acting like he's got nothing to be ashamed of."

Justin's cheeks flushed red and his eyes shifted from side to side as if looking for an escape. He didn't find one.

Cam continued and Beth couldn't tear her eyes from him.

"Justin seduced Julie. Set out to get her and he did. Got her pregnant and then tried to force her to marry him. He wanted into the Wheeler family," Cam said, voice dark and low. "He wanted her money. Wanted a piece of the ranch, and he didn't mind telling her any of it once he was sure she was going to have his baby."

Justin puffed out his chest and lifted his chin. "That's a lie."

Beth didn't think so. Glancing at the man now, she could see the truth etched into his hard features. She felt immediate sympathy for Julie. To have been used like that must have crushed her.

"It's the absolute truth and you damn well know it," Cam said.

"How could you do that to her? To *anyone*?" Beth asked.

Justin looked at her, and his mouth thinned into that straight, bitter line again.

"When she told Justin she was pregnant, he told her that she had to marry him." Cam looked the man up and down dismissively. "He knew Burt would be furious so he figured he had Julie trapped." Cam shot Beth a quick look. "But she wouldn't go along with it. She was scared to tell her father the truth, so she came to me."

Beth's heart hurt. For Julie. For Cam. For all of them. Well, everyone but Justin. "God, Camden…"

Apparently, Justin saw that Beth believed every word. He knew now he didn't have a shot with her, so he faced Cam angrily. "If you repeat any of that story, Guthrie…I'll sue."

Cam moved in on him. "You stay the hell away from Beth, I'll keep quiet about all of this. But not for you," Cam ground out. "For Julie. She doesn't deserve to be gossiped about. You did enough damage to her life."

"Julie was an idiot," Justin said, dismissing the girl he'd used and ruined. "If she'd just married me like I'd planned, none of this would have happened."

Beth sucked in a deep breath as Burt Wheeler stood up from a nearby chair. None of them had noticed him. But clearly he'd heard everything. Burt was trembling with barely controlled rage as he stalked directly to Justin.

"You did all of that to my girl. You bastard."

Justin backed up a step and bumped into Tony Alvarez. He was trapped, and the expression on his face said that he knew it.

Burt wasn't finished. "If I ever hear my Julie's name coming out of your mouth again, I swear by all that's holy, I will beat you into the ground."

Justin believed him. Beth could see that truth on the man's face. He backed away again slowly and Tony let him go. When Justin saw a clear path out of the building and through the crowd, he took it, crashing into people as he made a hasty exit.

Sympathy welled up in Beth's heart for Burt. The man looked as if his own heart had just been ripped from his chest. He took a shaky breath, then stepped up to Cam and held out his right hand.

"I was wrong about you, Guthrie. And I'm sorry for it. I'm sorrier still that my girl was too afraid to come to me when she needed help." His eyes were wounded, and Beth knew that he would be haunted by that knowledge for the rest of his life.

Cam shook the older man's hand and said, "Julie loved you, Burt. She wasn't afraid you'd hurt her. She was afraid of disappointing you."

Some of the pain in his eyes eased. "That's something, I guess." Burt sighed heavily and slowly shook his head. "I'm going inside to talk to James. I want to change my vote on your membership."

Nodding, Cam said, "Thank you, Burt."

He nodded. "You did right by my Julie. You took care of her and helped her when she needed it most. I was too blind to see that sooner, but I do now, and I thank you for that."

"That was kind," Beth whispered.

Cam was watching the older man thread his way through the people in the room. "He's not a bad man. Just a hard one."

Beth was silent for a second or two before turning on Cam. "You honestly thought I was 'with' Justin?"

He frowned at her. "You looked pretty cozy to me."

"So you didn't notice me trying to get away from him?"

"That's why I came over. I didn't like him touching you."

"Okay, I'm gone." Tony Alvarez moved away, leaving Cam and Beth alone.

Beth said, "Why haven't you called me all week?"

"You could have called to tell me you wanted to talk to me."

"Seriously?" Her jaw dropped. "I have to tell you that?"

People were turning to look. Everyone had missed the upset with Justin and Burt, but now they were paying attention.

"Damn it, Beth—" He grabbed her hand and led her through the crowd and out into the parking lot.

She had to hurry to keep up and didn't mind a bit. It was past time they talked. Really *talked.* Cam didn't stop until he was in a far corner of the darkened lot, where the shadows were deep and the nearby oaks dipped low enough to provide some privacy. A soft, warm wind blew past them and brought the scent of coming rain with it.

Beth didn't care. Lightning could have split the sky and dumped gallons of water down on them and still she would stand there, looking up into the dark chocolate eyes staring down at her.

"Look," he said tightly, "I waited a week. Gave you the time and space or whatever the hell else you needed, but I'm done now."

Her heart took another high leap. "Is that right?"

"Damn straight it is." He dropped both hands to her shoulders and pulled her close. "I get that you don't trust me. I'll earn that back if I have to work at it for the rest of my life."

She did trust him and would have said so if he hadn't kept talking.

"And, if you think I'm going away again, you're wrong. I'm here for good. And if I ever *did* decide to leave, I'd go nowhere without *you*."

Her heart was pounding, her breath coming in short, hard puffs, and she felt as if she could fly. Beth read the truth of his words in his eyes, in his expression, in the hard grip on her shoulders. "I believe you."

That surprised him. "You do?"

"Of course I do." She reached up and cupped his cheek in her palm. "I was done waiting, too. I was going to come to you tomorrow to tell you that I want you to marry me. I want us to have kids. Make a family. And live on your ranch just like we used to dream about, remember?"

He wrapped his arms around her, looked down into her eyes and said, "Why do you think that's the ranch I bought when I came home? I remember everything, Beth. And just so you know, I was coming to you tomorrow, too."

"Really?" She smiled up at him, and everything inside her settled into a warm glow that filled her so completely it should have been spilling from her fingertips.

"Really." He let her go long enough to dip into his jacket pocket and come up with a blue velvet ring box. "I drove into Dallas this afternoon. I wanted to have it with me when I asked you."

She took a breath and held it while she blinked frantically to prevent tears from filling her eyes and spoiling the view of the man she loved holding a ring.

"You have it with you now," she said softly.

"I have *you* with me," he countered, "and that's the most important thing. This—" he flipped the lid open, displaying a huge, square diamond flashing up at her "—is just a celebration of that."

Beth's breath caught as she looked up into his eyes again. "It's beautiful, Cam. It's perfect."

"Not until it's on your finger it's not." He lifted her left hand and kissed her knuckles. Beth felt that kiss all the way to her bones.

"I love you, Beth," he said, his gaze locked on hers. "I loved who you were then and I love who you've become. I don't want to spend another day without you. Beth Wingate, will you marry me?"

"Yes," she said quickly, and sighed as he slid that gorgeous ring onto her hand. She wiggled her finger and admired the flash and shine for a couple of seconds, then looked up at him. "I love you, Camden. I always have. Always will."

"That's what I needed to hear." He framed her

face with his hands and leaned in to kiss her softly, almost reverently. "You know, back in the day, I'd half convinced myself that I just didn't deserve you."

"That's ridiculous."

"No." He shook his head. "What's ridiculous is I almost let myself get convinced of that again."

"I never would have let you get away with that," she said, smiling as she leaned into him and laid her head on his chest, where she heard the steady thump of his heart. "We deserve each other, Camden. And we deserve the life we're going to make together."

"Darlin'." He pulled her back so he could give her a grin. "What a time we're going to have."

And then he kissed her, and Beth knew that this time they had both won.

* * * * *

Don't miss a single installment in
Texas Cattleman's Club: Rags to Riches!

Available June 2020 through January 2021!

The Price of Passion *by*
USA TODAY *bestselling author Maureen Child*

Black Sheep Heir *by*
USA TODAY *bestselling author Yvonne Lindsay*

The Paternity Pact *by Cat Schield*

Trust Fund Fiancé *by*
USA TODAY *bestselling author Naima Simone*

Billionaire Behind the Mask *by Andrea Laurence*

In Bed with His Rival *by*
USA TODAY *bestselling author Katherine Garbera*

Tempted by the Boss *by*
USA TODAY *bestselling author Jules Bennett*

One Night in Texas *by*
USA TODAY *bestselling author Charlene Sands*

COMING NEXT MONTH FROM

HARLEQUIN

DESIRE

Available July 7, 2020

#2743 BLACK SHEEP HEIR

Texas Cattleman's Club: Rags to Riches • by Yvonne Lindsay

Blaming the Wingate patriarch for her mother's unhappiness, Chloe Fitzgerald wants justice for her family and will go through the son who left the fold—businessman Miles Wingate. But Miles is not what she expected, and the white-hot attraction between them may derail everything...

#2744 INSATIABLE HUNGER

Dynasties: Seven Sins • by Yahrah St. John

Successful analyst Ryan Hathaway is hungry for the opportunity to be the next CEO of Black Crescent. But nothing rivals his unbridled appetite for his closest friend, Jessie Acosta, when he believes she's fallen for the wrong man...

#2745 A REUNION OF RIVALS

The Bourbon Brothers • by Reese Ryan

After ending a sizzling summer tryst years ago, marketing VP Max Abbott doesn't anticipate reuniting with Quinn Bazemore—until they're forced together on an important project. He's the last person she wants to see, but the stakes are too high and so is their chemistry...

#2746 ONE LAST KISS

Kiss and Tell • by Jessica Lemmon

Working with an ex isn't easy, but successful execs Jayson Cooper and Gia Knox make it work. That is until they find themselves at a wedding where one kiss leads to one hot night. But will secrets from their past end their second chance?

#2747 WILD NASHVILLE WAYS

Daughters of Country • by Sheri WhiteFeather

Country superstar Dash Smith and struggling singer Tracy Burton were engaged—until a devastating event tore them apart. Now all he wants to do is help revive her career, but the chemistry still between them is too hard to ignore...

#2748 SECRETS OF A PLAYBOY

The Men of Stone River • by Janice Maynard

To flush out the spy in his family business, Zachary Stone hires a top cyber expert. When Frances Wickersham shows up, he's shocked the quiet girl he once knew is now a beautiful and confident woman. Will she be the one to finally change his playboy ways?

YOU CAN FIND MORE INFORMATION ON UPCOMING HARLEQUIN TITLES, FREE EXCERPTS AND MORE AT HARLEQUIN.COM.

HDCNM0620

SPECIAL EXCERPT FROM

HARLEQUIN

DESIRE

After ending a sizzling summer tryst years ago, marketing VP Max Abbott doesn't anticipate reuniting with Quinn Bazemore—until they're forced together on an important project. He's the last person she wants to see, but the stakes are too high and so is their chemistry...

Read on for a sneak peek at
A Reunion of Rivals *by Reese Ryan.*

"Everyone is here," Max said. "Who are we—"

"I apologize for the delay. I got turned around on my way back from the car."

Max snapped his attention in the direction of the familiar voice. He hadn't heard it in more than a decade, but he would never, *ever* forget it. His mouth went dry, and his heart thudded so loudly inside his chest he was sure his sister could hear it.

"Peaches?" He scanned the brown eyes that stared back at him through narrowed slits.

"Quinn." She was gorgeous, despite the slight flare of her nostrils and the stiff smile that barely got a rise out of her dimples. "Hello, Max."

The "good to see you" was notably absent. But what should he expect? It was his fault they hadn't parted on the best of terms.

Quinn settled into the empty seat beside her grandfather. She handed the old man a worn leather portfolio, then squeezed his arm. The genuine smile that lit her brown eyes and activated those killer dimples was firmly in place again.

He'd been the cause of that magnificent smile nearly every day that summer between his junior and senior years of college when he'd interned at Bazemore Orchards.

"Now that everyone is here, we can discuss the matter at hand."

His father nodded toward his admin, Lianna, and she handed out bound presentations containing much of the info he and Molly had reviewed that morning.

"As you can see, we're here to discuss adding fruit brandies to the King's Finest Distillery lineup. A venture Dad, Max and Zora have been pushing for some time now." Duke nodded in their general direction. "I think the company and the market are in a good place now for us to explore the possibility."

Max should be riveted by the conversation. After all, this project was one he'd been fighting for the past thirty months. Yet it took every ounce of self-control he could muster to keep from blatantly staring at the beautiful woman seated directly across the table from him.

Peaches. Or rather, Quinn Bazemore. Dixon Bazemore's granddaughter. She was more gorgeous than he remembered. Her beautiful brown skin looked silky and smooth.

The simple, gray shift dress she wore did its best to mask her shape. Still, it was obvious her hips and breasts were fuller now than they'd been the last time he'd held her in his arms. The last time he'd seen every square inch of that shimmering brown skin.

Zora elbowed him again and he held back an audible *oomph*.

"What's with you?" she whispered.

"Nothing," he whispered back.

So maybe he wasn't doing such a good job of masking his fascination with Quinn. He'd have to work on the use of his peripheral vision.

Max opened his booklet to the page his father indicated. He was thrilled that the company was ready to give their brandy initiative a try, even if it was just a test run for now.

It was obvious why Mr. Bazemore was there. His farm could provide the fruit for the brandy. But that didn't explain what on earth Quinn Bazemore—his ex—was doing there.